PRAISE FOR MATTHEW McBRIDE

"Matthew McBride's new novel, *A Swollen Red Sun*, is rough and ready suspense, encompassing a wide array of characters from the sour side of life, and smashing them together with vigorous and blunt prose."

—Daniel Woodrell,
author of *The Maid's Version* and *Winter's Bone*

"The words practically vibrate off the page in Matthew McBride's amped-up and intricately plotted novel about meth freaks and dirty cops. Filled with scenes of both tremendous brutality and heartrending compassion, it is the best fictional depiction of the current drug epidemic raging across the Midwest that I have ever read."

—Donald Ray Pollock,
author of *Knockemstiff* and *The Devil All the Time*

"*A Swollen Red Sun*, simply put, is an epic piece of modern crime fiction. But within that, McBride never loses his sense of powerful intimacy with the characters, their lives, their families, and their demons."

—Todd Robinson,
author of *The Hard Bounce* and editor of *Thuglit*

"Memorable, unique, and at times, even haunting. Every character rings true from the feckless to the noble to the downright frightening. . . . [With] dark country humor, *A Swollen Red Sun* is a must read."

—Johnny Shaw,
Anthony Award–winning author of *Big Maria* and *Plaster City*

"Matthew McBride writes like a train doing 80 miles an hour towards a curve rated for 30. The doors are rattling, the couplings are screaming, and you're riding the blind, hoping like hell that the destination lives up to the ride. Which it does, and more. Matthew McBride is exactly my kind of writer, and *A Swollen Red Sun* is precisely my kind of book."

—Benjamin Whitmer,
author of *Cry Father*

"Matthew McBride is an American original. His dialogue crackles like a brush fire and he has a rare gift for pitch-perfect details that breathe life into each and every character. There's no other writer I know whose prose could sear paint off a wall."

—Hilary Davidson,
Anthony Award–winning author of *Blood Always Tells*

"Matthew McBride is one of those rare writers who can have you reeling in shock one minute, and laughing out loud the next."

—John Rector,
author of *Already Gone*

"Make no mistake, McBride is the king of Chainsaw Noir, and there's no one else who can step to the throne."

—Chuck Wendig,
author of *Blackbirds*

"Read [*Frank Sinatra in a Blender*] in a day. Loved it!"

—Charlie Sheen

A SWOLLEN RED SUN

To: Stacey Cochran,
Good Luck with
Eddie & Sunny, bro...

Matthew McBride
12/1/14

A SWOLLEN RED SUN

MATTHEW McBRIDE

MYSTERIOUSPRESS.COM

This is a work of fiction. Names, characters, places, events, and incidents either are the product of the author's imagination or are used fictitiously. Any resemblance to actual persons, living or dead, businesses, companies, events, or locales is entirely coincidental.

Cover design by Neil Alexander Heacox

ISBN 978-1-4804-8575-4

Published in 2014 by MysteriousPress.com/Open Road Integrated Media, Inc.
345 Hudson Street
New York, NY 10014
www.mysteriouspress.com
www.openroadmedia.com

For Jasmine Haslag[*]

[*]*Missing since 2007*

AUTHOR'S NOTE

I grew up in Gasconade County and I've lived here most of my life. Geographically, I've taken a few liberties with the landscape, but the places are real. The roads and the hills and the hollers, they're not on any map—but you can find them if you know where to look. It is a rural landscape of uncommon beauty.

On the other hand, Gasconade County has been called the methamphetamine capital of the world; in the 1990s, it was true. Maybe it still is. Yet, in this community, you'll find honest, hardworking people. They are teachers and farmers and factory workers.

But there are also a few lowlife degenerates. They are the ones I write about.

MM

Mount Sterling, Missouri

A SWOLLEN RED SUN

"The dawn came, but no day. In the gray sky a red sun appeared, a dim red circle that gave a little light, like dusk; and as that day advanced, the dusk slipped back toward darkness, and the wind cried and whimpered over the fallen corn."

—John Steinbeck, *The Grapes of Wrath*

PROLOGUE

They spent the afternoon butchering horses.

Reverend Butch Pogue drilled holes through the back legs and attached a contraption he'd built, then secured a metal bar above the hooves with bolts, and Junior pulled the tractor in low gear and raised the dead horse up in the great oak, where the Reverend skinned it out. Junior pulled the hide off in patches and sheets, and steam rose off the meat in waves of stench the Reverend found intoxicating.

They could buy cows cheaper than horses, but the Reverend liked horsemeat.

He laid yellow newspaper on an old wooden table and piled chunks of meat onto it. Then he hung a slab of meat on a hook that dangled from the rafter of a lean-to that sagged lazily from the barn.

A chunk of horsemeat had begun to spoil, and Butch wiped off a slick patch of mold with his palm. He ordered the boy to feed a wad of guts to the pigs.

The boy did as he was told as a gust of foul wind pushed the smell of blood toward the tree line and the hunting dogs began to bawl, the barks echoing over the treetops, down the side of Goat Hill, as the preacher slashed at the bounty that lay before him and flies crowded the pink slabs of meat.

The sun went down behind the mobile home like a burst of egg yolk that dripped from the sky and consumed the trees. Sycamores on the river cast long shadows in the burnt auburn hue, and golden shafts punched holes through plump clouds that looked ripe to carry wetness for days.

Woodpeckers knocked and pecked as spring water rose and swooshed through gullies and creeks, climbing their walls and swelling the ditches in low-country places, as the limbs grew plump with leaves and branches fought branches when the cool river kicked up wind.

Deputy Sheriff Dale Everett Banks stood beside the mobile home with a shotgun in his hands. He watched the windows for movement and listened for the sounds an old trailer makes when someone inside walks in a manner in which not to be detected.

"You in there, Jerry Dean? This is the Gasconade County Sheriff's Department."

Jerry Dean Skaggs was a convict on parole, for shooting a bald eagle, and a shit bum to all who knew him. He was violent, had a burly appetite for amphetamines, and was known to have a mean drunk-on come evening.

Deputy Banks pounded on the side of the mobile home. "Jerry Dean, I have a shotgun in my hands." Banks racked the pump action. "We need to talk to ya, bud."

Banks looked back at Deputy Bo Hastings as he circled the trailer with the strap of his Glock uncapped, his hand on the butt. He walked cautiously, with slow deliberate steps, heel to toe, tall grass spreading out flat beneath each polished shoe.

Both cops watched the windows. They heard only birds and wind and the approaching sound of an outboard motor humming between the bloated mudbanks of the Gasconade.

They met at the end of the trailer and exchanged doubts.

"Awful quiet in there," Banks said.

Hastings nodded.

"I'm gonna try the door."

Hastings knelt beside the trailer and looked below through the spacious gaps in the underpending, and everything he saw was covered in a dark coating of filth. There was an old bicycle and a cooler and a boat motor. Children's toys filled boxes that were damp from moisture and looked ready to fall apart.

Deputy Banks saw the doorknob turned freely, and he kicked the bottom of the door with his foot and nodded for Hastings, but

Hastings was already where he needed to be, his Glock drawn, ready to back any play Banks made with gunfire.

Banks went in first, the 12-gauge in front of him.

"This is the Gasconade County Sheriff's Department looking for Jerry Dean Skaggs."

Hastings followed behind Banks and walked down the short hallway with caution. He stumbled over toys until he found a small pink room. The drapes were stained brown, and what didn't hold stain had faded. Purple stuffed animals were sullied with cat piss. A litter box at the end of the hall overflowed with turds. Someone had written LITTLE BUDDY across the top in red marker.

Hastings found a portable cook stove and a cardboard box filled with lithium batteries. Another box held cans of ether and hoses and tubes. Hastings picked up a gallon bag filled with striker strips from old matchboxes and knocked over an empty Coleman fuel bottle with his shoe.

"Hey, looks like they been cookin' back here, Dale."

Banks walked into the back room, having secured the other end of the mobile home. His meaty hands relaxed their grip on the shotgun. "Find any product?"

Hastings said no, but now they had proof of what they had already known. Jerry Dean Skaggs was cooking meth in the child's bedroom of a dilapidated trailer home that was one step above being condemned or falling over—whichever came first.

Banks—a solid three hundred, with a plain, round face and heavy jowls growing from a wide, fat neck that sprouted from the gap of his shirt collar—turned to leave and his frame filled the doorway in full. The worn sheets of raw plywood creaked and split under his mass.

Hastings said, "Goddamn, Dale, don't fall through the floor."

The outside air was fresh and cool. It greeted them with the tang of river and fish, a scent both country boys knew, and one much better than the stench of a twelve-by-sixty-foot meth lab that smelled like ammonia and cat piss.

Deputy Hastings sat against the hood of his cruiser and chewed a mouthful of sunflower seeds.

Banks set his shotgun on the seat and grabbed a can of Skoal off the dash.

They'd taken the call together. They'd both been in the area, and Helmig Ferry sat a good half hour from nowhere. A deputy never knew what he might walk into. Backup was a good idea when it was available.

Skaggs had family in the hills and the huts and the trailers along the river. Spread out through miles of wooded hills and rock mountains. Country people connected by blood. They did not trust law and had no need for government. Money came hard, and the rural patchwork of Gasconade County was ripe with hillbilly chefs cooking meth wherever they could.

White-trash pharmacies run from beaten-down mobile homes at the end of dead-end roads would always trade pills for dope. A box of pills got you half a gram. The price you paid was having your name go on a list for the police to read.

Pills were hard to come by, and deals were made. People traded what they had for what they needed, but anybody who cooked methamphetamine needed anhydrous ammonia. Anhydrous ammonia was worth more than money—but pseudoephedrine was worth more than anhydrous.

You needed *both* if you wanted to cook good dope.

An aluminum johnboat with an outboard hummed upriver, and a man with a long oil slick of black hair and white skin and tattoos so bad you could tell they were bad from a distance turned to the right and tossed a cigarette into the boat's wake.

"Think that's him?"

"It's him," Banks said.

People from the hills were a cautious bunch; people on the river even more so. The sight of two cruisers parked at a trailer home meant somebody's kin was going to jail, and on the river it seemed like everybody was kin—one way or another—to everybody else.

"Only a fella didn't wanna be seen woulda looked away. 'Less he didn't see us," Hastings said.

"He seen us."

Hastings was a tall, lean kid with wide shoulders that stretched his shirts tight across the back and a chin strong enough you could pound on it for a while. His long, straight face was hard in the jaw. He was a cowboy who rode bulls until his dreams broke when a behemoth named Captain Sam threw him at the state fair and his back broke.

His daddy was a deputy before him, until he got his head

stuck inside a bottle. The name Hastings hung over the kid like a dark cloud. Weighted him down. He had ruts carved into his reputation and a lot to prove.

Banks picked up his radio. "104 to Gasconade Central."

"Gasconade Central, go ahead, 104."

"Gasconade Central, show me and 109 at Helmig Ferry, off Highway BB. Subject does not appear to be home at this time. Please advise."

Hastings looked at Banks as he drove a plump finger into the sweet black velvet and dug up a fat wad of Skoal and dropped it in his mouth and pushed it down behind his lip with his tongue.

"104, be advised, either yourself or 109 should wait. Otherwise one of y'all'll have to go back out tomorrow."

"Gasconade Central, this is 104. Thank you, ma'am. Will do."

Hastings looked upriver and held his hand to his eyes to shield them from the sun. "Well, what'll it be, boss?" he said. "I don't even see this guy no more."

Banks drew up a mouthful of spit and shot a long, juicy stream into the dirt.

"It don't matter to me none, Bo. Don't y'all got a ball game tonight?"

Hastings nodded. "We do."

"Well, go on, then. Get. See to it your old lady gets your drunk ass home in one piece after the game."

Hastings grinned and said, "Yes, sir." He wore his good-ol'-boy values across his face like a bad cliché as he left Helmig

Ferry and drove to Owensville to play softball with a bunch of other good ol' boys.

Banks moved his car from plain sight and parked behind a point of cedars. He checked his smart phone for a signal, but the reception at Helmig Ferry was touch and go. He played a game he'd downloaded, but his bratwurst-size fingers betrayed him at every opportunity until he finally set the phone down for good.

Banks tapped the Skoal and thunked the lid with a thick finger and packed it tight, then scooped out a pinch and a half to shove behind his lip.

The mist rolled in at twilight and cool air pushed a dense sheet of iron-gray fog in his direction as birds chirped above his head and the locusts squawked and hawed.

He realized the bedroom light was on when he turned to spit out the cruiser's window.

His head froze instantly where it was, and his hand moved to the gun on his hip. His eyes swept the area while the hair on the back of his neck stood rigid. A dab of juice coated his chin as he moved for the radio.

He thought of calling for backup but did not know if the light had been on or not. Bo had followed him out, but Banks did not know if the other deputy had turned it off. *Had he ever turned it on?*

Banks spit out the window without looking or aiming and thought about what he should do. *How long had he been sitting there?* Maybe he'd fallen asleep. It was calm, and the breeze embraced him through open windows in a lavish wave of sweet honeysuckle. Or dogwood. Whatever that smell was.

He removed the wad of snuff, which still had plenty of life, and flung it out the window. It was probably not worth checking out. He could leave. He was alone, and he was not getting shot by some tweaker.

Dale Everett Banks had one job: go home alive to his wife and kids. No one would blame him for leaving. No one would know but him. Leaving was the smart choice.

Banks considered sliding out the car's window so the light would not come on, but he knew he would not fit. He opened the door quickly. Turned sideways and stood up. The Glock in his right hand, he carefully, quietly closed the door and listened.

He thought about his partner. Hastings was sitting in Memorial Park, drinking cold Natural Light on the tailgate of a pickup truck with his cute wife painted on his side.

Banks drew in a bottomless mouthful of chilled air and turned down the volume on the radio. He walked and he listened. *Someone was inside.*

Banks felt his throat burn, and his heart slammed against his ribs in a way that was both appalling and invigorating. It was too late to call for backup. Deputies in rural Missouri worked alone. Always outnumbered and outgunned.

Come home alive. Those were the words cops lived by.

They waited on Highway K in an old Chevy truck with a two-tone yellow-and-white cab and a blue bed with no tailgate. One wore a red bandanna like a bandit, and the other wore a Halloween mask he'd taken from his sister's kid.

Jerry Dean Skaggs tapped his fingers on the wheel. Not because he was nervous, but because he had not slept in four days. He sucked a Winston through the mouth hole he had cut in the bandanna and concentrated on finding a sign of the truck through his binoculars. He thought about the cops who had been at his place earlier and looked over at his compadre.

"You with me, jack-off?"

Jackson Brandt wore a Darth Vader mask cocked to one side as he lit a small butane torch. He held the torch to a glass pipe, and together they watched the bottom fill with clear swirls of smoke. Jackson wet his lips then let off the torch's trigger and welcomed a bowl full of chemicals into his lungs.

That first breath of fresh dope was revitalizing. His thoughts began to whirl inside his head; slowly, he set the pipe down on the armrest and melted into the battered seat cover.

"Gimmie that, Jackson." Jerry Dean pulled at it.

Jackson looked at him. "Huh?"

Jerry Dean was broad across the chest and covered in jailhouse graffiti. His nose was wide and bent from countless breakings and bustings. His eyes were set low under his brow, the left quick to wilt, but both were brown and vacant and capable of limited emotion.

He pitched his butt out the window and exhaled, then returned that spent breath with a clean hit of crank that pierced his reality like a hollow-point round.

Both tweakers kept to themselves, thought boundless thoughts, and made plans of all the things they promised themselves they would do but never would—things they would build if they just had time, and they *did* have time, had nothing but time, except the habits of a meth cook were sporadic, depending on what project he worked on between batches of dope—and these projects varied from one task to another in various stages of completion, since no sooner did a meth cook start one thing than his mind would fire off vital, superlative orders for the body to follow, which it did, at least it tried to, but often the need and desire and compulsion was outweighed by the strong pull to sit in a cool, safe place with plenty of windows and smoke speed, watch for people, and wonder when the front door of your mobile home would blow off its hinges from a battering ram—because the same customers who drove a hundred miles for fresh dope were the first ones to tell the cops where they bought it when they got pulled over on the way home.

Jackson asked Jerry Dean if he was sure about this thing that they was about to do.

Jerry Dean looked up. "Don't start in with that pussy bullshit. It's too late ta pull out now."

"No, it ain't."

"Oh yes, it is. That old bastard'll be roundin' that corner in a hot minute. You best get your head right. Make sure you can drive this truck."

"My head *is* right J.D., and you know I can drive this truck. Long as this piece o' shit don't break down."

Jerry Dean looked over, balled up his fists. "Them's fightin' words 'n' you know it. It's a goddamn Chevrolet."

"Whatever, man. Just hand me that pipe."

Jerry Dean handed Jackson the pipe and he sprinkled powder in the bowl and struck the torch and inhaled the smoke. They waited for the old man to come.

Olen Brandt spent the day on his Allis-Chalmers tractor, feeding hay in round bales to the cattle on his 240-acre ranch outside of Mount Sterling. The weather was backward in every way that it could be. One day, it rained and got cool; the next, it was hot and sticky, the humidity a wet veneer that coated his aged and withered body with cold sweat. Even in summer, he kept a flannel at arm's reach.

It was hell getting old. Things that used to work didn't. Things that *did* work barely worked at all. His hands throbbed and took turns falling asleep. Lately, his bladder was failing him. He always had to piss, but when it came time for the pissing, the urge left as quickly as it had come. Sometimes he was too late and wet himself before he got off the tractor. He'd been forced to take precautions.

"Don't worry," his doctor said. "You're eighty-one years old. Feel lucky you can still drive a tractor."

But that was easy for *him* to say. He was *thirty*-one. He wasn't the one in diapers.

"Come on, girl," Olen called to his Australian shepherd, Sandy, and closed the gap to the bottom forty. He pulled the homemade fence across gravel, the one he'd built twenty-five years ago with barbed wire and old posts. "Come on, girl," he said again.

Sandy was getting up there in her own years, but the one comfort Olen took was knowing he would go before she would. That was one less body he would have to put in the ground. One less face—animal or human—he would have to say good-bye to.

At the same time, those particular thoughts grieved him the most. Kept him up at night, long after he should be in slumber. If he died, what would happen to his girl? His Sandy. She was all he had left after he'd lost Arlene to cancer.

He had one departed son, waiting with his mother, and another son as good as dead: locked up in a cage he might never get out of for a crime he surely did.

Olen climbed back on the tractor and slipped the long handle forward, easing off the clutch, and she purred, smooth, and black diesel smoke poured from the pipe as he goosed the throttle.

The hill ran steep and rough with knots and undergrowth and fathead stumps, some rotten and dead, but strong. Olen followed his usual path with Sandy trotting behind as the sun spread wide to his right with swaths of butter-yellow patches and bursts of pink flavor among blue.

The skin stretched tight over his smoke-gray jaw, and silver hair lapped above his ears. What little hung over blew when the wind came.

When he reached the peak and the rough ground became smooth, he eased up on the lever and worked the gas, and the diesel relaxed, but the smoke pipe still pumped an oil cloud that the wind took and fed to the sky.

Sandy ran to the chicken house, as was her custom, and chased the last two wandering hens into the small abode where they roosted. Olen pulled the tractor into the building and stopped in the doorway. He peed in the dirt as the sun disappeared behind his barn.

He should have been gone already. Had to pick up two tanks of anhydrous ammonia from Cuddy's Farm & Supply. Should have left an hour ago, but he got preoccupied in the low bottoms. Cutting brush and fixing fence. He'd make the run tomorrow. Get there in early evening, have plenty of time to visit his old friend Tom Cuddy.

It was late. Olen was tired, and he could not see worth a damn at night.

He closed the shop doors, then met Sandy at the chicken coop and closed his girls in.

"Good night, ladies."

Then he saw his stud rooster in his spot, head under wing.

Beauregard was the biggest, most spitefully malicious rooster in Gasconade County. A powerful Brahma just shy of knee height and a solid twelve pounds. Olen should have peppered him with birdshot years ago but could not bring himself to do it. He had no need for a rooster, but Beauregard's strange personality kept him spared. Insurgent, renegade behavior and attitude radiated from his authoritative struts and scratches, and Olen came to find the fowl avant-garde and eccentric in ways he never thought capable in poultry.

Beauregard was more of a guard dog than a rooster. He would not let visitors out of their cars. He would attack the UPS man on the rare occasion that called for one to arrive. He had attacked a surveyor and a veterinarian. He once attacked a county assessor—a glorious act that made Olen proud.

Olen stood outside when company arrived and did his best to act surprised when it happened, but Beauregard was a master of stealth, and it was only a matter of time before he showed up ripe to ambush.

Olen Brandt was a farmer who loved his tractors and his land. He'd developed a strong appreciation for the little things life gave back. Small, unnecessary observations that remain useless until you are old. The little things only a fool would enjoy.

It was the love of a good dog and the hate of a bad rooster that kept him alive.

Deputy Banks climbed the steps to the sound of blood pumping in his ears, and it blocked out everything else but the warmth that spread across his cheeks. He banged on the front door and hoped he didn't fall through the porch.

"Gasconade County Sheriff's Department. Open this door *now.*" He smashed the door with his left hand. Glock in his right. "I'm comin' inside, I am armed, and I swear to God I'll shoot, so don't make me do it."

Banks threw the door open, then stepped back and waited for action that did not come. He produced his Maglite and held it in front of him below the gun. Scanned the dark room and reached up with his left arm and found the switch. Banks reminded whoever was listening he was armed. Said he was prepared to shoot and meant it. Warrant or not. Justified or not. He'd rather be judged by twelve than carried by six. He was not going to die in a mobile home that smelled like cat shit.

Banks flipped the switch and the room filled with cheap thirty-watt light. The only thing Banks knew was adrenaline. Pumping hard. Rushing through his veins. His mind was a series of dull mechanical throbs that vibrated in waves and bursts in a uniformed rhythm. *Whomp! Whomp! Whomp!*

His mouth spoke words he could not hear over the sound of his heartbeat.

Banks kicked the toys and the stuffed animals out of his way and took hard confident steps to the kid's room. He might find Jerry Dean high or drunk. Or he might find a twelve-year-old with a handgun.

A cat sprang into the hall causing Banks to jump, and the floor shook hard, maybe even the whole trailer, as the cat ran back to the bedroom where it came from.

Banks looked down at the litter box filled with fresh coil-shaped droppings and kicked the box hard—sent it into the wall—in a powerful explosion of gray rock-turd dust. He took a deep breath, feeling both relief and disappointment.

Still, he could not let his guard down. Getting in was half the battle. Now his mind switched gears, sped up; he got to thinking about all the ways this could end. Jerry Dean might be on the front porch, waiting.

Everything had happened fast. He hadn't had time to think.

Now, he was thinking. He remembered the car was unlocked. Key in the ignition.

There was a shotgun on the front seat, loaded and ready to fire.

Banks looked down at the cat and swore. He should have just left when he was able.

When Banks turned to leave, he saw several packages on the floor, wrapped in clear plastic, wrapped tightly with rubber bands holding them together. They'd been buried in the bottom of the litter box that he'd scattered across the floor.

He knelt down and looked closely and saw that it was money. Thousands stacked in bundles wrapped in plastic.

The deputy tried to move, but his shoes had bonded with the floor. Banks strived to take it all in but had to focus on the fact there might be a man outside he would have to kill who stood between the mobile home and the police car.

Then he did the first thing anyone would do. He got down on the floor and rooted through that cat shit. He'd seen big wads of cash before in similar situations. He'd seen a drug bust at Cave Hill that netted more than a hundred thousand. But that was a few years back, and this looked like more, or at least just as much, though it was impossible to tell at the moment.

He scooped it all up before he could think to do otherwise, all that he could find, and shoved it in an orange and black duffel bag that said GO DUTCHMEN!

He took deep breaths and pushed the fear aside. Focused. Walked from the bedroom and stepped out the front door and took quick strides to his car.

He knew he was wrong to do it but could not stop. It was too easy to justify why he deserved the money more than Jerry Dean, a tweaker cooking meth in a child's bedroom.

Banks tossed the duffel bag on the front seat. The shotgun was still there. Keys where he'd left them. Skoal on the dash.

He vacated Helmig Ferry as the night came and didn't see oncoming headlights until he got to Bay, a town of maybe thirty-five people. He radioed Gasconade Central and told them to show him off the clock.

They said be careful. See him tomorrow.

He ignored the nervousness inside him and drove to the only place he could think of to hide the money.

Bo Hastings hit two triples and a double before the pain in his back became so great he had to take to the bench. He was sweating profusely from the Percocet he'd taken before the game.

Bo's back had snapped like a dry piece of kindling when that beast drove his hooves into his spine. He never should have lived. Never should have walked if he did live.

But Bo was a survivor with a champion bloodline that went back four generations of law enforcement. The call was an inevitable one he'd fought his whole life.

After the accident, being a cop was all he had left. He was a broken man with limited options, and the shoes he was meant to fill were clearly defined by each generation that wore them—his father being the generation that ruined the legacy his grandfathers worked so hard to create.

Bill Hastings kinked the chain in a way that could not be unkinked.

"You OK, babe?" Becky wrapped her arms around her man, but he pulled away.

"I'm sweaty, hon."

She smiled and said she didn't care. Said his sweat was sexy.

Then she laughed. Loud and infectious. Her friends laughed, too. The high school volleyball coach patted Bo on the back and told him he had his hands full.

The man who owned the lumberyard grinned and walked up to the plate.

All of them laughed. Everyone loved Bo Hastings. He was the all-American boy.

They smoked crank until it got too dark to see what was burning and what was scorching, and finally admitted to themselves that the old man wasn't going to make the run. Jerry Dean blamed Jackson. Told him he should have known.

"How would I know? I'm sittin' here with you, ain't I?"

"Cuz he's *your* uncle?"

"Yeah, well, ain't no need ta remind me 'bout that, Jerry Dean."

The old Chevy cranked slow but finally turned over, and Jerry Dean smashed the gas pedal. The lifters rattled as the old truck lurched from the woods and crawled up to the asphalt. Jerry Dean clutched it, found second, and the worn-out bastard coughed and sputtered, then pulled strong like a good Chevy ought to.

He had a mess on his hands if they did not get those tanks. The kind of mess a man got hurt over if things went wrong. People he ran with were hard people from the hills and the woods. He had partners to consider.

Jerry Dean Skaggs dealt with a family who cooked crank with the anhydrous he supplied. Strange knoll dwellers from Goat Hill. A hard vicious man named Butch Pogue who was violent and cruel. More so than Jerry Dean had ever thought to be.

Butch had killed a man once. Done time for it. But he found the Lord in Algoa and had repented of his sins. Now he called himself a reverend, though Jerry Dean thought that was far from true.

Jerry Dean knew he was wading in the devil's pond with Butch Pogue. Even the deputies didn't venture up Goat Hill without good reason.

He hit third and wondered if he should go back to his trailer. His boat was upriver at his cousin's, the place Jerry Dean parked his truck in case he had to run.

His day had gone to shit in a hurry once he'd seen those pigs at his trailer, but even with a busted door, they could not go inside. Not without a warrant.

He wasn't concerned about the stash in the litter box, either. Not even a cop would look there.

They drove back roads to the sounds of Jamey Johnson bawling through the speakers, and Jerry Dean reached for a half joint in the ashtray. He looked at Jackson and dusted off the roach. "We gotta make some kind of move if he don't get them tanks."

Jackson shook his head.

The radio lights blinked and the CD player died momentarily, then returned to life, and the cab filled up with a quick burst of orange. Jerry Dean lit the joint and puffed a few quick hits to get it going. He took another and handed it to Jackson, who ignored it.

"Take it." Jerry Dean held his hit up high in his chest. Jets of smoke shot from his nose as he spoke and held his breath at the same time. "C'mon, take it."

Jackson reached for it, and Jerry Dean pulled it away.

"Fuck you, then."

Jackson knew better than to arouse the demon inside Jerry Dean. He'd split Jackson's lip into a bloody mess last week with a hard fist. Jackson knew Jerry Dean was quick to anger when he was drinking or tweaking. Knew some things were best let go.

Jackson finished his beer and threw the can out the window. He slipped his mask down over his face and watched the cherry glow to his left. They rode back to town with sparse conversation.

Olen poured a cup of strong coffee and watched long dandelions bend and sway in the fields below the window. The east was yellow, and it welcomed the day with promise. Particles of dust and dog pelt swam in the hot air he passed through as he stepped onto the porch.

His hummingbirds fought and ate and hummed. He watched them have conversations without words. Just tweets and pecks and squawks that told stories he would never know.

The air tasted like corn smelled, and the ground was a blanket of leaves. A pair of Canadian geese flew above the house, and Olen smiled. Wished he had back all the things he'd lost through the years. Some memories were miles away, but others never left. Memories of her, in the garden: pulling and picking and raking and hoeing.

Her beautiful hair, when it was blonde and wavy, with full curls that bounced off her shoulders like velvet springs. She went shorter as the years passed, then grayer. Then it was gone, and she was not the same Arlene he had loved for fifty-nine years, four months, and eighteen days.

She was a small, frail skeleton with loose skin, and part of her died in his arms every day. But Olen held her hand until the end. She was tormented with intolerable pain. Yet all he could do was watch and cry and wish that God would take him instead of her.

She died on a Tuesday morning.

He woke up in the recliner the hospital had placed beside her bed. There was a doctor and a nurse in the room. The machine was loud, and the sound it made was flat and continuous. He knew that she was gone. She had waited until he fell asleep before she left him.

He did not cry; he just looked out the window until the room was empty. And then it was the two of them. Him alive and her dead. He should have held her hand when she disappeared into that heavenly void, but he'd been sleeping.

He never had a chance to say good-bye.

Olen lost a war with emotion and stared through the glass. There was hard rain and wind and a sky filled with light, but he never saw a rainbow.

Deputy Dale Everett Banks woke before the sun and walked out the back door to piss. The wind was cool. It came from the east in a constant push and brought with it the first weak specks of light.

He'd stayed up until 2:00 a.m. Couldn't sleep. Woke up twice to take leaks—not that he couldn't have waited; he just wanted to come outside and stand there. *Think*.

He felt bad about the money. Drug money though it was. He'd stolen it, and that knowledge played hell on his conscious. One way or another, he had to give the money back. But he *couldn't* give it back. Or *wouldn't* give it back. He had tough decisions to make before things went wrong. Country people, dirt-poor from birth, did not lose that kind of money, even to the law, without trying to get back what was taken.

When Jerry Dean came, and eventually he would, Banks had to be ready.

After the obligatory pot of coffee, he packed his first dip of the morning and went to the back porch to watch the golden orange sun crest slowly. Bacon frying and hard snaps of fat and grease popping in cast iron called him from the kitchen.

They'd bought an old cabin of rough battered logs and fixed it up over five long years of weekend remodelings and countless vacations spent cutting cedar. They hammered and hung drywall and ran electrical and did plumbing. Added two rooms on back and a laundry, with a loft above it all where they watched the stars at night through a skylight window.

Everything felt right when Banks closed his eyes.

"Dad, Mom says c'mon in here. Breakfast's ready."

Banks nodded, sucked that last tuft of minty black for all it was worth, worked it dry, then dug it out with the tip of his tongue and let it fall in a spent clump on the grass. "Tell 'er I'm comin', Jake."

Jake was fifteen and soon to be driving, with a strong interest in farming. He wore Wranglers and boots. Knew how to gut deer and change oil. He could drive a tractor and clean a shotgun. He worked as hard as a boy his age could and made his daddy proud.

They ate breakfast in a hurry. Steph was texting. Reminded her mother she'd need hair spray. Jake reminded them both he had a school trip to Kansas City for the FFA. Had to have his money turned in by Friday or he couldn't go.

"How much you need again, boy?"

Jake was hesitant to say. He knew they didn't have it to give.

"Hundred dollars," he said, and swallowed hard.

"Hundred dollars!" Banks yelled. "Goddamn."

His wife stopped what she'd been doing and looked at him with the same tough eyes she always did when he swore in front of the kids. "Dale *Everett*," she scolded.

Grace laughed her precious little laugh. Her laughter was the sound of paradise. The sound angels made. The laugh a father could love more than anything else in the world.

She was eating the jelly off her toast and she looked up with red cheeks and soft blue eyes.

"Hey, pumpkin," Banks said.

"Dah-dee!"

Grace was the love of his life. She was born with disabilities, but they worked with her every day. Jude quit her job at the courthouse to give Grace what she needed, and it was hard on her, hard on everyone. But after the first year, they saw the improvements they had feared with all their hearts that they would never see.

Now six, she was so alive with her words and observations. She was slow, but amazing in all the ways that special kids are. She took nothing and gave back love and smiles.

Banks loved his family enough to die for them. He would take money that wasn't his from a meth cook to give them a better life. He would send his kids to college and invest in their futures. It was a cold, hard world beyond their small farm. So that was the least he could do.

Jake looked at his father, curious and guilty for wanting.

Banks winked and blew his angel, Grace, a kiss. He told the wife he was sorry about what he'd said and then told Jake to have a good time in Kansas City.

The boy exploded with raw bliss that only a fifteen-year-old boy would know. Jude gave Dale a look that said *we don't have a hundred dollars*, but Banks took everything in with warm eyes. Told his wife they'd make do. Told his family he loved them but he had to go to work.

"Catch some bad guys today, Dad," Jake said.

"Bye, Daddy," Steph followed. Her eyes never left the phone.

He gave his Grace a kiss on her tiny strawberry lips and did the same to Jude.

"We gonna be all right, Dale?" she whispered.

He said they'd be just fine. Told Jude to be sure and get Steph her hair spray.

He left the house and went to work. Already wondering if he'd made a mistake, and choosing to believe he hadn't.

• • •

Banks met Hastings by the antique water fountain that was known to give cool water with rust.

"How'd you do last night, kid?"

Bo said he hit three home runs and a double.

Banks told Hastings that was bullshit. Asked him how many beers he'd had.

"Relax, boss. Had the old lady drive me home."

Banks smiled. Hastings was a good kid. Big and strong with a bull head and an iron will. His old man had been a good cop but could not hold things together. Started drinking hard, harder than a man should drink when he wore a badge. His paperwork got sloppy; he started boozing on the job. Then he would drink behind the wheel. Some knew; some didn't.

In the end, he made a bad decision and saved everyone the trouble of pretending.

"That tweaker ever show up last night, boss?"

Banks took a drink of hot coffee and cussed. "Huh?"

"That tweaker? Meth head with the bad tattoos."

Banks swallowed more hot coffee. He felt awkward and could not look at Bo. He shrugged and said he never saw the man.

"Guess one of us'll be goin' back out there at some point."

Banks changed the subject. "Don't you have court?"

"Yep," Hastings said. "Never fails."

Banks told the kid he'd see him around and left the station. The kid left for court.

• • •

The Gasconade County Courthouse was perched high above the Missouri River on a towering stoop of land outside Hermann. Its dome roof and mural paintings adorned the inside and the familiar smell of old dust greeted Hastings.

A deputy's life was a life of inconvenience, often testifying several times a month.

Hastings left the station by a quarter of ten, bound for his date with court. He'd pulled a kid over for speeding in the spring. Thought nothing of it. Just assumed he would let the boy go with a warning. Never figured the boy would run. But he did. He waited until Bo was beside his truck and then dropped the hammer. When he did, the ass end jumped to the left and almost hit the deputy.

Bo dove out of the way, reached for his gun on instinct, but stopped. Had to think for a minute. He could not believe that little son of a bitch had run.

Hastings jumped into the cruiser and ran codes. Lights swirled in red and blue and sirens cut the afternoon silence as the engine raced and screamed across the Christopher S. Bond Bridge.

But the chase was short-lived, and the kid wrapped his truck around a box elder tree. Not hard enough to kill him, but hard enough to throw him out a window. Hastings called for an ambulance and waited. When they searched the kid's truck, they found a small baggie of meth and enough pot to twist a joint. Not enough drugs to land him time but enough to draw five years' probation.

Hastings sat down in the courtroom and waited to be called and tried not to fall asleep.

• • •

Banks wanted to swing out past Helmig Ferry and see Jerry Dean. Wanted to know what he'd be dealing with. Jerry Dean could not report the stolen money, but he *had* seen cops at his place. Assuming that was him in the boat. Banks knew it was.

By noon, Banks was on the other side of the county. He was on his way to a call about stolen car batteries when an Amber Alert went across the radio about a missing high school girl. It was the kind of call that precedes other calls.

Banks remembered her name, Summer Atwood. She had disappeared from Franklin County after the homecoming football game. A friend dropped her off at a commuter parking lot, where she'd parked but was never seen again.

At the time, it was big news. It still was. Sightings had been reported off and on for the last few weeks. None of them proved real. A lot of high school girls looked alike.

"Gasconade Central, this is 104. Am currently in the area of New Haven, by the Franklin County line. Please advise."

A call had come in. She'd been seen at the Fuel Mart at the south edge of town.

"104, this is Gasconade Central. Please be advised we have 105 en route."

Banks reached for the mic attached to the top of his shirt. "Gasconade Central, this is 104. Copy that."

Banks let off the gas and grabbed his clipboard to restudy the address. Back to the less pressing issue of the missing car batteries.

• • •

Jerry Dean Skaggs spent the morning watering the plants that paid his bills. His cash crops grown along the Gasconade River were scattered and strung out in small intimate clusters. Nurtured on the south side, among the cedars and inlets that jutted and poked out of banks that made narrow passage.

He walked a half-mile through itch weed and dense timber with a wooden pole across his back. It stuck out a good four feet beyond each shoulder, and every two feet there were large brass hooks where he'd hang the four five-gallon buckets it took to provide drink.

He walked a different path each time to avoid creating an obvious trail for some hunter to stumble across and follow. There were many different kinds of hunters in the woods. Deer hunters and coon hunters and turkey hunters. *Even pot hunters.* People just like him who poached other growers' crops. Jerry Dean would know about that. Jerry Dean had been known for crop poaching.

Farmers and pot rustlers who knew what they were looking for were always a threat, but a good cultivator with strong survival instincts *used his head* and was not afraid to put the work in.

That meant walk and crawl and carry.

Jerry Dean carried water over rough country. Up rocky hills and down deep hollers. Brought nourishment to his plants. Crops grown in places hard to reach. He'd pick the last place he, himself, would venture, places a man would not explore without good reason. Then he'd work the dirt with a shovel and mixed chicken shit with the soil.

Thorny patches of locust thorn worked best. A man would have to be curious indeed to crawl through spiky jagged locust thorn. Sharp as knife points and they gave deep cuts that burned like a napalm fire.

Jerry Dean crawled through many feet of sharp prickly points and edges, which gouged and sliced and stuck him. But he worked through it. *Determined.* Four days strong on crank. He was hard at work at his livelihood. Growing good weed. Better weed than those other peckerheads around similar parts could manage.

It was high-grade Afghan Kush he and his partner, Bazooka Kincaid, sold in bulk to the coons in the city. They funneled the weed down a pipeline courtesy of Jerome Delmont, a spook he'd met in Algoa.

It was tumultuous at first, but they'd grown close—driven together by circumstance—and a trust formed, groomed slowly over time, until they bonded as cellmates do.

Jerry Dean made his rounds to the *girls* and removed the lids from the buckets and gave them the nourishment they needed. His shoulders ached, and he dipped in the river to wash the funk off. To wake him up and give him a clean face for the twenty-minute boat ride back to the trailer. He would sleep it off at his cousin Ronnie's. He did not want to deal with pigs. He'd check his money later; it was fine.

He needed half a day's rest but managed to stay conscious long enough to pass out in the small cluttered bedroom of his cousin's trailer without air-conditioning.

• • •

Fish stirred outside his mobile home. Shirtless and lean-muscled. Wearing sullied jeans with a hole in the knee and a pair of cowboy boots. It was a hot day for October. Eighty-two degrees. He walked to his small shed and opened the door and stepped inside. There was a window unit working overtime, but you couldn't tell. Water ran down the wall and soaked an extension cord that ran out the door and stuck in a utility pole.

"It's hotter than two rats fuckin' in a wool sock out there."

Jackson Brandt nodded absently. He was propped up against a toolbox on an old kitchen chair. There was a lightbulb in his hands. Sweat running down both cheeks onto his neck.

He'd punched out the center of the metal ring and dumped a handful of salt in the bulb. He held his thumb over the hole and shook the bulb vigorously. Specks of salt removed the white kaolin stain on the glass.

He screwed the lid from a plastic soda bottle over the threads. There was a hole at the top he'd fitted with the hollow tube of an ink pen.

Jackson worked slowly and methodically. He was heavily involved, thoroughly engaged at the deepest level of concentration. Lightbulb pipes were delicate to construct and difficult to maintain, but they were the best pipes for smoking crank if you had the patience to make one.

Fish set a plastic Tupperware container on his makeshift workbench and opened it and removed a large bag of crank. He looked at the glass pipe beside Jackson.

"That bowl cashed yet?"

Jackson stared at his hands, lost in thoughts Fish dared

not attempt to contemplate. Fish kicked the leg of Jackson's chair.

Jackson looked up, startled.

Fish pointed to the pipe and asked if there was a hit left. Told Jackson he had all day to make that lightbulb.

"Sorry, man. I'm on it."

Jackson set the lightbulb down and put the pipe to his lips and held a torch to the bottom. A small cloud of smoke formed inside the bowl like a miniature tornado. Both were entranced, mesmerized by its beauty.

Jackson, watching it, waited until just the right moment, turned off the torch, and inhaled the smoke.

He leaned back against the toolbox, and Fish took the pipe from his hand so he could think. Fish held it to the light and studied brown stains from the scorched meth.

The shed smelled like sweat and crank.

"Fish?"

Kenny Fisher's wife walked out the trailer's back door, tired and frustrated. Or so she would have them believe.

"Shit," he said.

Fish set the pipe inside the container and snapped the lid on tight. "I do *not* wanna hear her bitch." He handed the container to Jackson and pointed to an Igloo cooler.

Again she called him.

"Whatchya want?"

"I'm runnin' to Walmart. Then I'm gonna pick the kids up from Mom's."

Fish nodded. "OK, then. G'bye."

He turned and closed the door and nodded for Jackson to return the crank, which he had just placed inside the cooler beside another, larger bag of crank.

Jackson returned it and bit his thumbnail and waited for another bowl.

Fish took the container and removed the lid and picked up the bag. It was white, with a subtle touch of bronze when the light hit the rocks. Carefully, he pulled a small chip that looked like ice from the bag and dropped it in the glass bowl. They were smoking the latest product Jerry Dean had cooked up with the Reverend.

Fish was a former associate of Jerry Dean and still helped out with the smurfing. Sometimes he cooked. But he was also a good customer. He would take the crank he bought—always pure and clean and better than any crank he had ever seen—divide it, remove half the bag, and crush up vitamins to replace what he'd kept.

Fish would *cut* the meth with the pills, *step on it*—and the crank was so good he could do it and still make money *and* retain an abundance of product for himself.

Fish held the pipe up to the window and lit the bottom with the torch and watched it fill with smoke. He let off the torch and took a slow pull—which was cool to his lungs and mouth—held it longer than he had to, then let it out and stared out the window. His thoughts immediately beginning to take hold of him—thoughts and observations. His shed was a mess. He needed to clean it. And he *would* clean it. Just as soon as this bowl was gone.

Then he looked out the small window at the mess that had

become his yard. Dead grass and broken tree limbs and half a dozen cedars trees that had to go. And, now that he thought about it, there was a tree behind the mailbox that could go as well. It was the neighbor's tree—but that didn't matter. He'd be doing him a favor, way he saw it.

There was nothing Fish couldn't do on crank.

Jackson reached for the pipe. Told Fish that shit was good.

Fish nodded. Said it was the best batch yet, which was the same thing he said about every batch.

The two smoked crank and talked and thought. Jackson Brandt chewed his bottom lip with chipped brown teeth, teeth that had not seen a brush in weeks—*months*. His lip was red and raw and looked plenty painful. But Jackson kept chewing anyway.

Fish asked Jackson, "Ever get the feelin' you know somethin' 'bout somebody," he paused, "but they don't know you know?"

Jackson, suddenly nervous, shrugged. Stared down at the floor.

Fish, standing beside his workbench, looked down at Jackson. "Come on, now. You ain't never had a feelin' somebody was doin' somethin' behind your back . . . and they *think* you don't know." Fish pointed to his temple. "But you do—*you know*."

Jackson agreed, though somewhat reluctantly, and unsure where the conversation was heading, reached for the pipe and held it to his mouth and lit the bottom. He took quick puffs until smoke jetted from the end, then lowered the torch and drew a long, slow breath from the pipe and held it. Closed his eyes and let the gray smoke bleed from his lips and go up into his nose and into his eyes and float up into his mess of straw hair.

There was a look in Kenny Fisher's eyes that scared Jackson. Made him wish that just once he could smoke crank with a regular guy. A guy without uncertain eyes or bad tattoos or body odor. Or maybe just someone who wasn't fucking crazy.

"C'mon," Fish said. He leaned down, slapped Jackson's shoulder.

"Let's go for a ride."

Olen worked the ancient tiller with calloused hands and a strong back, and the sun bore down and reddened what skin was left exposed after long sleeves and a wide-brimmed shade hat hid the rest. He let the machine do the work, and it turned the rough dirt into smooth, manageable soil. His garden would boast peppers and tomatoes of every shape and size, and cantaloupe and watermelon and sweet potatoes.

The dirt was worked into fine moist powder as he handled the machine and made rows wide enough to stand between. By 1:00 p.m., he took lunch, which was a ham sandwich and a bottle of Coke. Then he crawled onto the antique bed in the spare room where he took his naps. Arlene had called it his sleeping bed. Once Olen hit seventy years old, he found he could not make it through the day without recharging.

He was drawn to the bed. The one his boy had slept in every night for all of his eight years.

By 2:30, Olen was awake and had a pot of strong coffee dripping not a minute later. A half hour after that, he was feeding cows and moving them from one field to the next. He pulled the silver pocket watch from his bibs and checked the time. He had business in town to tend to, but he also had the last ten acres of the bean field to turn up by weekend. Tonight it might rain.

Olen studied the sky. Rechecked his watch. He could make a dent in that field if he started now. If he left by five, he'd be home by dark.

He called out to Sandy and pulled the Allis-Chalmers from the tractor building. Hooked up to the plow and raised the hydraulics and passed down the hill. Sandy ran ahead and then slowed down. She still had the heart to run, but she did not have the legs to carry her.

He crossed a slab that separated the low bottom from the thirty-acre patch of corn he'd combined, and Sandy found a spot beneath a pecan tree. Olen climbed down and ran his fingers through the dirt. It was dry. He looked up at the sky. Soft and blue with fat clouds.

Olen spat and climbed back atop the Allis-Chalmers and set the plow down in the lower forty and started cutting earth. Let his mind wander. These moments were the best he had left. Every field he plowed could be his last.

Olen knew that and respected it. Things you acquire on this earth are meaningless once you're alone, and memories become the currency of choice.

Growing old is the most painful thing in the world.

Jerry Dean could not sleep with the sounds of doors slamming and kids yelling and babies crying. He stumbled from the bedroom and told his cousin's wife she ought to show those crumb-snatchers a little belt leather every once in a while.

"I should, huh?"

"Best thing you could do."

She flicked ashes into an ashtray that had started overflowing six months ago and everyone in the trailer had decided they'd grow the pile.

"Ever think about cleanin' up around here, Darlene?"

Darlene was married to his second cousin, Ronnie. She was in her mid-thirties with a thick, corpulent body, cantaloupes for tits, and four kids who ran around the trailer unsupervised while she sat in her recliner and ate and chain-smoked and dreamed of all the places she could be but there.

"Well, ain't you just an expert on child raisin'?"

"I know I got thumped on plenty by my mama."

"Yeah, and look at all the good it done."

Jerry Dean stood there covered in a dripping gleam of sweat.

"Nobody likes a smart-ass, Darlene."

"Well, nobody asked you to come to my house and sleep in my bed now then, did they, Jerry Dean?"

He shook his head. "Where's that brother of yours? I need to see him."

Darlene had a brother named Ray who was twice her size. He was a guard at Algoa, and the key to another one of Jerry Dean's business ventures, the middleman who smuggled in product for Wade Brandt to distribute.

Wade Brandt was getting out soon, and that was something they should talk about.

"I ain't seen him," Darlene said.

"What about Ronnie? He out playin' chef or gatherin' pills?"

"How the hell should I know? Ain't seen him, neither."

"Cut the shit, Darlene. You always know his whereabouts, so don't play ta me like you don't."

"You're so smart, why don't you figure it out."

Jerry Dean rolled his eyes. "Woman, how that cousin of mine puts up with you I'll never know."

"Fuck you."

"Oh, you'd like that now, wouldn't ya, darlin'?" He stepped toward her and reached down and squeezed one of her big, sloppy tits.

Darlene slapped his hand away. Told him to get out before she told Ronnie what he'd done.

Jerry Dean walked to the kitchen and opened the fridge. "You be sure 'n' do that, sweetheart. You tell him what mean old Jerry Dean gone 'n' done." He grumbled and gagged, then hacked up something from deep down and spit yellow in the trashcan. "Got anything ta drink in this shit hole?"

The bottom of her broken-down recliner slapped shut, and Darlene jumped to her feet, a GPC cigarette clenched tight between her teeth. The floor shook as she stomped from the living room. "You get the hell outta my kitchen."

Jerry Dean held up a finger and nodded his head. He drank milk from the carton, and his sweat ran down the side.

Darlene started laughing when Jerry Dean realized the milk he was drinking had gone to sour and he spewed white chunks into the sink and dropped the plastic jug on the floor.

Darlene stopped laughing. "That milk went bad two weeks ago when the power got shut off. That serves you right, you dumbass. Now get out!"

Jerry Dean nodded and pulled his long, greasy hair from his mouth. "I'm goin'."

"And don't come back."

One of Darlene's brats sat on the arm of a second broken-down recliner, and Jerry Dean shoved him off backward and he made a thump on the floor.

"I'll be back tomorrow," he said, and walked out the door.

Jerry Dean looked up to an indigo sky filled with mushroom clouds while he motored down the Gasconade River and burned a joint. He did not care if the cops were waiting at his place or not. He'd had four hours of sleep. He was as good as gold.

Jerry Dean secured the boat and smoked his roach down to nothing and pitched it in the river. He weaved through a maze of debris and car parts until he got to the front door and stepped inside. The place smelled like cat shit.

"Goddammit, Little Buddy," he said to the runt of a cat.

Jerry Dean saw the litter box turned upside down before he even closed the door. "No!" he yelled, and stomped down the hall.

His money was gone. Not that all of it was his—it was to be split between himself and his associates. Jerry Dean had just been holding it, waiting until the man he took orders from told him what to do.

"You crooked sons-o'-cocksuckers."

Jerry Dean kicked Little Buddy when he walked up to rub and sent him airborne across the trailer. "You motherfuckers!"

He punched a hole through the cheap wall and his fist came out the other side. Buried his arm to the elbow in pink insulation.

It was all gone. Fifty-two thousand.

Jerry Dean hollered and cussed and punched more holes. He'd been robbed by the cops. The two from yesterday. Jerry Dean paced and swore. His partners would never believe him.

The fat cop had been Banks. Jerry Dean knew of Banks. A Southern Baptist shithead, but no thief. It must have been the young one who found it, the cowboy.

Jerry Dean walked back to the box and crawled through the litter for a second time, and his heart sank. He would not survive without the money. It was the bulk of their profits from a drug-smuggling operation that funneled meth inside Algoa. They were depending on it. Everyone was. If Jerry Dean had lost their money, then he was as good as dead.

Fish followed his wife from afar, in Jackson's minivan, thinking she wouldn't recognize them if they got too close—which they had on occasion—but Raylene broke speed laws with reckless abandon and swerved from lane to lane. Failed to use her turn signals and talked on the phone.

Fish was angry. He complained about the windshield. Shattered in the middle with a thousand cracks and no glass on the driver's side.

"You could fix this with a scrap of plastic," he said.

Fish badmouthed Jackson for his laziness. The wind in his face through the missing window was hot for the moment, but sure to drop toward frost-level by midnight.

Jackson kept quiet. Which made things worse.

Fish, overflowing with nervousness and uncertainty, grew a sick feeling inside his stomach.

Jackson, in the passenger seat, held the pipe in his palm tightly, content with his thoughts as he looked out the window at the fields of cut cornstalks on dirt slabs of earth. Windshield full of dust.

Jackson's mind was slow from years of crank and he was easily misled. Jerry Dean knew this. So did Fish. But Jackson was a gatherer; he was resourceful. He knew where to find things no one else could.

When he'd hooked up with Fish, they'd met at a pharmacy where they'd both been buying pills. There'd been a mutual curiosity between them. How each knew exactly what the other was buying, and why. How, within minutes, they would be in their own cars, pulling bent sheets of tin foil from under the seat. Lighting it and smoking it. Needing just one hit before they drove to the next store.

They were slaves to crank, powerless to its illusions, and before Jackson knew it, they were smoking crank together. And then they were cooking it and selling it. Running with a hard-hitting crowd of convicts and bikers, caught up in a scheme delivering crank to Algoa, to a crowd that scared Jackson more than he let on.

But he just wanted dope and was quick to follow their lead, with little regard where it took him.

Raylene took Highway A to Highway Y, but she never did go to Walmart. She turned past Hog Trough Road instead, and crossed a washed-out section of driveway toward the brand-new double-wide of his cousin, Earl Lee.

"Oh, God, that whore," Fish said. Tight-jawed, teeth gritted. Knuckles bone white under clear pink skin.

Jackson, in his own small world, kept silent, with an indistinct awareness of his surroundings.

Fish found the prospect of his cousin and his wife outlandish. Earl Lee Ramsey was a car salesman who drove a six-cylinder Mustang with a siren glued to the dash. It belonged to the dealership, but he said it was his. He thought nobody knew.

But Fish knew. Knew his cousin Earl Lee was without credit, and whatever credit he did have was bad. *Early*, as they called him, was a volunteer firefighter when he wasn't selling Fords, and though he *did* live on his own patch of land, in a brand-new double-wide, Early mostly lived off the government—and if his wife had been fool enough to run to him, well, then, fuck her. Early could have her.

But then Fish got to thinking. About the way Early had looked at her when they'd been together. Not that he didn't look at all of them—at every woman—but the way he looked at her was different. There was something about the way his eyes hadn't left her. How they followed her from room to room.

At the time, Fish hadn't noticed, but now it was apparent. There'd been a hunger in the both of them that only the bonding of flesh could gratify.

Fish loosened his grip on the wheel, which was bending. Kept thinking. About the way she'd looked at him back. She'd smiled. Laughed at his jokes—and then there was Thanksgiving. They'd been drinking and snorting lines, and for one reason or another, his wife and the girl his cousin brought with him had flashed their tits.

It was a very good night, which they had all enjoyed. An evening filled with yard bird and crank. Holiday memories they would always cherish.

But the way Fish now remembered it was different. His wife had been behind it. He knew it. She had orchestrated all of it just for him. For Early. And the more Fish thought about that night, the more he thought about everything.

He smoked crank out of Jackson's pipe and thought, until finally, Fish had come up with a plan to fix them both—especially the cousin. You *don't steal from kin*, and his cousin should have known that. Some things weren't worth the price you had to pay in the end—and this price was a bit on the steep side. Even if she was a whore.

Fish fell apart inside as he drove. He would be alone without her. His parents were gone. Everyone who had ever loved him was gone. Except Raylene. And by the looks of it, she was gone, too, though Fish was bound and determined to prevent that from happening.

Kenny Duane Fisher had gone by Fish for as long as he could remember. His mom called him Fish. Even his dad, when Fish was around, though Fish was sure he used worse names when he wasn't.

They'd lived on the edge of town, by the county line. His

mom cleaned houses, and his dad sold tires. His parents did their best to provide, but his old man had a way with the back of his hand that would find Fish beside his jaw.

It wasn't that he didn't love him, but that he didn't know *how* to love him. That's what his mom had said. But his mother said a lot of things, and Fish learned long ago what to believe and whatnot to, though it was not her fault and he knew it.

It was his father's fault. Or it was God's fault.

To this day, he didn't know which. He didn't know what to think or who to blame. But a part of him died in a hayfield back when they were kids. It was the last good year of his family's life—because the Fishers shared a burden that was hard to let go of.

It was easier to forget.

Fish had a sister who died when she was six, but the family never talked about that. Some things were best unsaid; at least that's what his mom had claimed—though for weeks after the funeral, she set Karla's plate at the table, until Big Fish set her straight.

"She's done in the ground, Mary Ann. What you're doin's just makin' things worse."

"But I miss her."

Big Fish grunted with a nod of understanding and forked a load of beans in his mouth. Big Fish got to drinking after that, even more than he had before, and then the bottle became his family, and any quality of life they had previously known was gone.

• • •

Fish returned to his driveway. Lost in thought. Filled with pain and wired from meth. He would not permit Raylene to leave him. Or take his sons or their home—assuming the bank didn't take it first. They were a half-year behind, and Bay Bank was threatening to reclaim. Fish swore he'd catch up, but Ms. Dixie made a habit of following through.

Fish would smoke crank and think about the ways he could turn things around. For weeks, he'd had a cooler full of product to sell, but that never happened. Now it was too late.

He thought about his wife and his cousin, and those thoughts birthed hurt, the deepest he had ever felt. It metastasized within him, until the hurt that became anger had become cancer, and it surged through his body like electricity, killing everything that lived inside.

Fish had known a lifetime of pain, but this cut was the deepest. *The perfect end to a miserable life.* He could hear his father say. When he closed his eyes, he could see his dad, working on their farm. Pall Mall between his lips and a cold one in his hand.

It was summertime. Dad was cutting hay on his old John Deere tractor. In the fields, making rounds. It was noon, and it was very hot. Wind a blanket of searing moisture.

Mom sent Little Sister to the field to fetch him. But Dad hadn't seen her walking.

That year had been a good year for red clover. It grew freely and abundantly along the hillside. Pecan trees lined the field to the north and beyond. To the west, a wall of oak stood proudly. It gave shade that covered half the field, but not until late evening.

That was the summer red clover grew tall. Taller than the

fences that sagged between old posts that ran up and down hill-sides and through crooks and swags and fields and woodland. That hay was as tall as she was.

And then she had tripped, and he did not see her. Sun in his eyes.

The shriek could be heard clearly over the sound of the machinery.

He'd smashed the brake pedal with his foot and turned the key back. Cut the power to the PTO. Wanted to believe it was a stump he'd hit, but her screams cut as sharp as any razor.

Big Fish had jumped down and turned white. Could not move or breathe. He had run her small body through the haybine.

She was still alive, but she was silent. He could not move her. She'd been cut to pieces, one arm slashed off. Blood poured from her handless wrist onto the dirt.

Big Fish reached into the machine with his arms to hold her. He touched her and loved her and told her he was sorry.

When his wife ran out the door, she was screaming. But she stopped when she reached the gate and projectile-vomited in the yard. She was not the same woman after that day, and Big Fish was not the same man.

Once Little Sister became a memory, everything in their lives changed.

Dale Everett Banks stood at the edge of the garden and watched his son and daughter pick tomatoes. They had row after row of Big Boy and beefsteak and heirloom, Brandywine and Black

Cherry and Boxcar Willie—three hundred plants that took two hours to pick, four days a week, but it kept Jake and Steph busy. Even young Grace did her part.

"Everyone has a job to do," Jude said. It had been her mother's saying, and the first time she'd used it had shocked her. *I have become my mother*, she told Banks, who laughed. *Well, then, I guess I've become my father*, he'd said. Then she laughed. Told Banks he'd been his father since the first day they'd met. She asked him if he still remembered.

"How could I forget?" he'd said. They'd been at a bar called the Blue Star, where Banks's dad played music. It was a small place with smoke-stained walls and a beer-stained floor. His father was a drunk named Everett Roy Banks, and he'd played a mean banjo when he was sober, and a piss-poor banjo when he wasn't.

But that night, he was abstemious and his playing was electric. It was a memorable performance if ever there had been one.

Banks sat down in a lawn chair and opened a beer and thought about life. Watched his children and his dog and his wife. Jake picked each tomato and gave it to Steph, who took it and blew her hair out of her face and set it *gently* in the box she carried.

Dale Banks was a family man—because that came first—and then he was a farmer and a deputy. But between those last two it was a close tie for second.

Jude was beside the house, on her knees, pulling weeds that threatened the daylilies in her flowerbed. She made a large pile, and Grace, their angel, filled her pink bucket and set it in her wagon and pulled it to the edge of the yard.

These were the moments Banks lived for. Moments that moved too quickly—and he knew it—so he watched these moments closely. Took the time to record those images in his mind. His kids had the life he'd always dreamed they would. They worked their small farm and had jobs to do and pets to feed. They had *responsibilities*. Something every kid that age should have, but didn't.

Meat cooked on the grill of the fire pit. He'd built it as a project with the boy. The whole family helped out. Scoured roadsides and creek beds. Built a solid pit with chunky rocks and mortar and a fat chimney that billowed sweet smoke when the cedar chips burned to embers.

Banks walked to the pit and poured Natural Light on his steak. The meat seared and popped and deep fragrant whiffs blew from the chimney and filled the air with a succulent fog that engulfed the table.

The steaks smoked and sizzled and the aroma was deeply pleasant. It was suppertime. Almost dark.

Jake had homework to do and cows to feed.

Steph would go inside, disappear behind her laptop. Banks knew this and accepted it. She was growing, and he could see it. Getting older, and filling out her curves, curves that troubled Banks. But what could he do?

Banks just grinned and raised his can and took the final drink. His life was a blessing. His daughter would be in college soon, his son right behind her—or maybe he would go to tech school. Or maybe he would farm. *Don't get ahead of yourself, Banks*. Jake still had a few more years. He was still just a pup, and still trying to talk Banks out of his Bronco. *But, Dad, it's perfect*, he said. Though Banks was not convinced.

"Your dad loves that old thing," Jude told Jake. Which was true, Banks *did* love that old thing. It was built back in 1979, when they still made a car from steel. It was dented and dinged, but it was tough and strong and it started every time, as long as you pumped the gas pedal when you turned the key.

Jude went to clean up while the kids finished picking. Jake carried boxes to the garage, and Steph approached Banks. Lip out. "Daddy, this sucks," she said.

Banks shrugged. Told her she didn't know how good she had it.

"Girl, when I was your age—" He stopped himself abruptly. Thought about what Jude had said and didn't know whether to stop talking altogether or to continue.

Steph rolled her eyes and finished his sentence and made the decision easy.

"Yeah, I know, Dad, I know. You picked tomatoes every single day—thousands of them—and green beans and potatoes."

Banks put his arm around his daughter and squeezed her.

She squeezed him back.

"Guess I told you that one, huh?"

She looked up at him and smiled. "About a million times, Daddy."

"A million and one," Jake walked by and yelled.

Banks tossed his empty beer can at the boy, who sidestepped it.

"Damn, boy. With moves like that you shoulda played football."

"Well, I was just sayin'."

"Well, nobody asked you."

His wife brought out plates and glasses and set them on the picnic table. Steph went inside for a jug of tea.

They sat down at the table and talked and prayed. Ate beef they'd raised, with vegetables they'd grown. It was a picture of a life he'd imagined twenty years ago, when he made Jude Camper his wife.

Being a deputy and having a farm, those were the things that mattered. Raising your children right. Teaching them and loving them.

Steph was texting while Jake dug a splinter from his finger with a pocketknife. Gracie was drinking juice and singing. Buster, their beagle, licked his lips as he walked up to Banks.

Banks, casually, and with a stealth that was surprising, dropped a small chunk of meat beside his foot for the dog to find—an act he had forbidden his children to do on numerous occasions.

When he looked up, Jude smiled and shook her head. She had caught him.

Banks grinned back and shrugged.

The guilt of what he'd done was subsiding. *Moments like this*, he reminded himself. He thought about the duffel bag and the money. About the consequences and the fallout. But now his daughter could go to college. To a real school. And Jake would need a pickup soon. Jude could use a trip to Branson; she deserved it. The years since Grace was born had aged her.

But Jude smiled and worked hard and loved her children, and that's what Banks loved most about her.

Goats clanked horns and fought in the pasture while Banks absorbed his family's love.

The sky was pink and orange and cloudless as evening settled over the cabin.

The Dodge turned over, and Olen looked at Sandy in the passenger seat. She wagged her tail and licked the window. Most dogs rode in the bed of the truck, but not Sandy. She demanded to ride up front with the old man, and the old man was happy to oblige.

Olen had spent the afternoon plowing the wheat field and tending to various brush fires he'd started. By quarter of five, the old truck found pavement and scrolled over the blacktop at no more than forty-five miles an hour. He traveled back roads with little traffic. Passed shacks and trailers and alfalfa fields shaved clean of hay.

He drove Highway K with time to spare. Tom Cuddy would be at the store until seven.

Olen liked Tom Cuddy. They went back to the days of the old one-room schoolhouse in Mount Sterling. Tom had lost his wife to cancer, too, in the summer, so Olen knew they would have much to talk about. He looked forward to their conversation. Tom could probably use a good handshake.

Olen parked the Dodge and walked inside and was disappointed to find a young man on a cell phone behind the counter who did not look old enough to shave. He set his phone down when he saw Olen and offered a polite smile. Asked how he could help.

The old man scanned the room with troubled eyes. "Where's Tom Cuddy?"

The young man looked uncomfortable. Tried to shrink down inside his shirt. "Mr. Brandt, I'm sorry to tell you this, sir, but Mr. Cuddy passed."

Olen was shocked. "What the hell're you talkin' about?"

The boy put his head down. Said it happened two months back. Told him again that he was sorry.

"*What* happened two months back?" *Had Tom gotten cancer, too?*

The boy wanted to walk away but Olen would not let it go.

"Tom Cuddy shot himself, Mr. Brandt. Again, I'm awful sorry to hafta be the one to give you this God-awful news."

"Shot himself?" Olen refused to believe it.

"Yes, sir, with a deer rifle."

Olen walked outside where Sandy waited and she licked his hand.

Tom Cuddy shot himself. It was unbelievable. How long since they'd talked? He thought about it hard. Time had a way of passing you by and made the days blur and run together. It had been a good year since they'd last spoke. He knew Vera was sick, but he did not know how much time she had left.

But Tom was lucky and she went quickly. Or so he'd heard.

Olen thought about poor Tom shooting his brains out with a rifle. Thoughts Olen knew well. You could place the rifle butt against the wall and press the barrel to your head. Steady it with your left hand. With your right, use a stick to push the trigger.

"Come 'ere, girl." Sandy licked his face, and Olen walked back inside. Settled up.

The kid met him out back and hooked the trailer to the receiver hitch of Olen's Dodge. It was a long trailer. Tandem axle. Hauling two one-thousand-gallon nurse tanks of anhydrous ammonia. He told Olen to be careful. Told him again he was sorry. He knew Tom Cuddy was a friend.

Olen nodded. "The last one I had left."

Olen moved the truck across the parking lot and rolled back down Highway O. Overhead trees shaded the road and dim rays of light shone through.

He shifted gears, and the Cummins diesel pushed dark smoke across the shoulder. Olen could not draw his mind away from his friend. Tom could not live without his wife. His partner. He wondered what a man's last thoughts might be just before he pulled the trigger.

Olen heaved the load in fourth gear through the straightaways and kept his rpm running high, where the power was. He turned onto Rural Route F, made a right turn at the next split, and followed. He saw a wild turkey spring from a clover field and take aim for the trees, but he could not shake his thoughts of Tom. He wondered if he'd taken his shoe off and used his foot. Surely, a man could push the trigger with his toe if he had to.

He came to the gravel pile the state used for rock, and a beat-up Chevrolet jumped from the ditch and onto the road.

Olen jammed the brakes and yanked the shifter out of fourth and into third.

"You son of a bitch." The trailer whipped back and forth while he fought to hold the road.

The truck in front died suddenly, and Olen stomped his brake again and brought the Dodge to a hard stop as the anhydrous tanks rocked and shook and threatened to break loose from their cradle.

Olen put the truck in neutral, his foot on the brake; his heart had stopped beating a half-mile back. He set the emergency brake and opened the door. Sandy walked to the edge of his seat and barked. Olen yelled out, asked what in God's name was wrong with them? It looked like they'd shot out of the damn woods.

He stood beside the Dodge and waited for the door to open on the Chevy. There was just enough light to see a man behind the wheel.

Sandy came to his side. Growled and barked.

"Calm down, girl."

Jerry Dean ran from his place in the woods. He came up behind the old man and clocked him in the back of his skull with a Desert Eagle.

Olen went down in a heap of limbs. Sandy growled. When she sprang for Jerry Dean, he shot her. She yelped and fell beside the old man and died on the concrete.

Jerry Dean jumped behind the wheel and the truck lunged forward and pushed coal-black smoke into the night, smoke that painted the air with an oily haze above a tired old man and his dog.

• • •

Banks sat at the picnic table and drank beer and looked toward the edge of his property and watched orange coals turn white hot as blue flames jumped and tussled in his fire pit grill.

"Honey, Bo 'n' his wife might swing by for a beer."

"Oh, that's nice," Jude said.

"Hell, I still got good fire. We got any o' that corn to throw on?"

Jude was pretty sure they did. She'd look. Then she asked about Becky. "How's she doin'? Poor thing."

Becky Hastings had suffered a miscarriage in the spring. But Bo hadn't brought it up, and Banks hadn't asked.

"Guess she's fine," he said. Jude knew that was the best answer she would get. Men did not confide the way women did. They should, but didn't. Especially cops.

"Well, I hope they're able to make it. They're sweet kids."

Banks said he knew. Hastings was the best rookie out there. Gifted with natural instincts and confident—not too confident, smart enough to know too much confidence would get you shot. Bo Hastings had a name to make for himself, and the future was there for his taking.

By twilight, Banks sat with Hastings at the edge of the yard that overlooked a fifteen-acre tract, covering both field and wood, most fenced but some open. Enough land for goats, a few cows, and a handful of chickens. They grew crops, which they'd just harvested, and though they had not brought much, every bit of income helped. Brought the cost of life down by a couple of bucks and taught his kids the value of the land.

Life was about hard work, and Banks made his kids work hard when they were young so they'd never know anything but.

The two deputies talked more like friends than coworkers. Banks had eighteen years in the department. He'd seen them come; he'd seen them go. But he knew Bo Hastings came from good people. *His* people. Raised up in the country. They lived off the land and tried to do right by God.

The wives talked about the things wives talk about when husbands meander off to do their dealings, and Jude saw pain in Becky's face so she asked about the miscarriage.

Becky looked down, said it was sad. "We never had time to name it." Said somehow being nameless made it easier to let go of something that was never hers to keep.

"I do have good news, though," she smiled. "You'll hafta wait until Bo tells Dale."

Before Jude could respond, Grace waddled up to Becky and handed her a doll with blonde stringy hair and a red dress.

"Bay-bee!"

Becky smiled and pinched Grace's cheeks. Grace raised both arms. "Up."

Jude laughed. Said that was her latest thing.

Becky hoisted Grace up in the sky and she giggled. Then Becky kissed her little cheek, and Grace kissed back. A big, uncoordinated kiss with an open mouth. The kind of kiss a baby gives.

The deputies returned and grabbed new beers from the cooler. Banks asked about that corn-on-the-cob.

"Ready, hun."

Jude had rounded up a few freshly shucked ears and thrown them on the grill and cooked them.

"Y'all hungry?" Banks asked.

They took their seats around the picnic table, and Banks said a few words of thanks. He thanked God for the bounty He'd bestowed upon them. Thanked God for their health. He did not thank God for the money, though he ought to.

"In the name of Jesus Christ, we pray. Amen."

Jerry Dean followed Jackson to a gravel road south of Hermann and pulled over on the shoulder to have words. He walked up to the Chevy. Saw Jackson was worked up.

"Now, this is 'bout as far as you go, man."

"What happened back there, you fucker?"

"What?"

"You didn't never say nothin' 'bout no guns. We ain't never even talked 'bout havin' guns, J.D."

Jerry Dean stood on the gravel and faced Jackson as he sat behind the wheel. He took a step to the door, bent down. Said, "Well, *excuse* the fuck outta me, Jackson Brandt, if I don't wanna be attacked by no goddamn dog."

"Well, you sure as all hell didn't have to hit the old man."

"That were a love tap, is all. Reckon he'll be fine."

Jackson looked ahead through the windshield, his jaw flexed. All he'd wanted was crank. He never wanted to see nobody hurt. He cared about his uncle. Though he hardly knew him anymore.

He turned. Met Jerry Dean's gaze. "That dog wouldn't've hurt you none. She's as old as he is."

Jerry Dean took a deep breath and a step back. "Listen, I ain't got time for this bullshit from you, man. Case you forgot, we got a stolen truck with two thousand gallons of product just sittin' here on the side of the fuckin' road. Now, get my truck outta sight. Take it ta your place. Just don't go gettin' nosey 'n' followin' me."

"Why the hell not? I ain't gonna sit this out. Not after already bein' a part of it like I am."

"Cuz you don't wanna go where I hafta go, Jackson. . . . *That* I can promise you, man. I swear ta you, there's men done been up Goat Hill that ain't never come back down."

Jerry Dean's words sent a powerful message. The Pogue clan was dangerous. They were private people who did not venture down the hill or leave the woods.

Butch Pogue was a monster that fashioned himself a preacher of his own religion. A polygamist of sorts who took wives and corrupted them with his teachings. Goat Hill was a compound and a prison and a world of many tortures. That much Jackson knew.

Jerry Dean walked backward toward Olen's truck. "Go on, numbnuts. Skedaddle."

He climbed in the Dodge and left his associate sitting on the shoulder.

Jerry Dean put fire to a doobie and pulled the tanks to the far west corner of Gasconade County. Mostly back roads of hard gravel and red dust. He drew long, slow hits from the joint to calm his nerves.

The Pogue clan and their brood were known but not spoke of, and when so, only in calm voices and hushed whispers. They were people who came from the dirt. Generation after generation of warped, misguided ways handed down through beatings and teachings that became more twisted and immoral with each passing. Every generation worse than the one it followed.

Goat Hill was a small mountain of solid rock that opened to a few hundred acres of wood and fields at the top where the Pogue compound flourished.

Valentine Ford sat at the base and surrounded the entrance to the hill like a rolling moat. The back of Goat Hill was a high bluff of boulder and stone. There was one way in or out, and the path twisted and turned over battered earth that only the tallest and strongest vehicles would survive.

The road ran hard and rough with potholes and washboards dominating the stretch that led to the hills. The far end of the county had few people but the Pogues and their kin, so the county did its best to stay away.

The passage had deep canals carved into rock that washed loose for the first time a hundred years ago and more washed away with each rain.

Deep chunks of missing road and grooved rock festooned his course as the Dodge bounced through holes and the trailer wiggled and jerked—but Jerry Dean tugged in low gear, the truck doing all the work and the joint glowing red hot with each potent draw.

Butch Pogue made the strongest crank Jerry Dean had ever seen. Beautiful dope that burned clear and clean. The Reverend took his time. His measurements accurate and precise. He took great pride in his product.

The preacher respected the flame and the temperatures and the volatile elements he worked with. He prayed for his batches to burn clean and strong with the heat from a thousand suns. Blessed them with rituals and sacrificed pigs and dogs.

Jerry Dean had seen him do it. Heard of him doing worse.

The Reverend ran strong on pure, clean crank for days and days without sleep. He groomed his dogs, then fought them against one another and preached to his wives and son—long fervent sermons packed with fire and brimstone chants during which he'd shoot pigs with arrows and fire shotguns into the sky.

He wrote his own scripture and was fond of quoting it to those chosen few who felt his call. The rumors were they'd consumed people. Fed the guts to the pigs. Burned the skin and crushed the bones and ate the meat.

When Jerry Dean reached the ford, the hills were alive with sounds of pitch-black night. Long continuous urges and wild callings of birds and bobcats and coyotes.

Valentine Ford sat low between two rock walls of Ozark granite with conduits blasted from the sides by the hand of God that kept the creek well fed and swollen. The ford was dense, ran many feet deep, and was impenetrable in even the slightest hint of rain.

Jerry Dean dipped into the chilly water and the engine hissed and he felt the slight rock of the cab when the truck settled down. The water hit mid-door, then climbed higher until the headlights went dull under white water.

Jerry Dean put the Dodge in four-wheel drive, and both shafts twisted hard and moved the big truck through to the other side. When the nose climbed out, he hammered down and hoped the tanks wouldn't float off the trailer.

He climbed the steep rise toward the peak of Goat Hill, and the sky got close but stayed dark. The moon was a small chunk of cheese behind black fog that shrank and expanded between cloud pass.

Farther up the road, he came to the first of several ramshackle dwellings. Some looked to be lived in and others abandoned, but he was hard pressed to guess which was which. What Pogues still alive were on the hill or in Algoa, and it didn't much matter to Jerry Dean, or anyone else, who was where.

To his right sat a combination of what was once a single mobile home but over time became three. What yard he could see was a burial ground for appliances. Old stoves. Washers and dryers. There were bullet-riddled barrels in the yard next to a heap of scrap metal. Off in the woods sat a graveyard of historic cars and a bundle of white PVC pipes that varied in length.

He swerved around a mountain of roofing shingles that looked to be new and was probably stolen. On the other side of the road was a small shack that caught fire long ago but had since been remodeled using mismatched sheets of tin and plywood that warped in the weather. A rusted Oldsmobile with the roof caved in and the windows busted out was parked in front.

He found more ruts and knotted humps of rock as he pulled through the hills and the hollers. Air cool and dank. Jerry Dean finished the doobie and put it out with slobber and swallowed it in a gulp. Wished he had a beer to enjoy but the preacher loathed beer. Said it was the devil's piss and was quick to induce slothfulness and lethargy.

But Jerry Dean did not see how a man who made crank would care. How a man who beat his wife and ate horsemeat would have a problem with alcohol in the slightest. But he did. The Reverend had a big problem with alcohol.

Once Jerry Dean told Butch the disciples in the Bible drank wine, but Jesus never did no crank—and he saw right quick what a terrible mistake that had been. A fool of a thing to say to a man who believed he had a direct, undeviating pipeline to the Almighty.

Butch reacted swiftly and pulled a straight razor from the front of his bibs. Held the blade against Jerry Dean's trembling Adam's apple.

"You swine," the preacher said. "I demand a blood atonement for this blasphemy." Jerry Dean saw the face of the devil that night. Saw two dead sockets with black pools of snake's blood and breath that smelled like meat.

Jerry Dean reached up and felt the scar that ran five inches in length across his collarbone where that crazy son of a bitch had cut him.

Butch Pogue had assured him he was there to do God's work, and Jerry Dean begged for forgiveness. Not from God, but from the man with a blade against his jugular. When Butch let him go with a flesh wound across his shoulder, he told Jerry Dean he was lucky, and Jerry Dean knew it to be true.

At the top of the ridge, the decaying old house came into view and gooseflesh broke loose under Jerry Dean's tattoos. It was a two-story farmhouse made of wood and rock, and the roof slanted hard to the left, like it would fall to the ground if a man tossed a rock on it. The back of the dwelling butted up to a slope that ran steady up the ancient tree line to a crooked utility pole as old as the house.

There was an antique coal chute under the living room window surrounded by ranks of wood, some split, but most green and drying in the sun, waiting to burn.

Nothing grew in the soil but weeds, and the flowers were black and wilting. The grass was dead, scorched by the heat. Everything on Goat Hill was dead.

Banks drank eight beers, about four more than he should have, and Hastings got tanked as well. They'd spent the evening talking guns and car chases. The night before, another deputy, Scotty Winkler, had found himself in a good one. He clocked two guys on sport bikes going over 140 and decided to chase them down.

They tore out Highway 28 westbound. One rider pulled over, but the other guy ran—and instead of being happy with what he had, the deputy got greedy. Wanted the one who'd run. Winky gave the best chase he could give, but his sedan was no match for the motorcycle.

Winkler drove the Impala so hard the light bar blew off the roof and dangled by wires. Both riders got away and everybody laughed when Winky limped back to the station with his sirens secured by duct tape.

Once Bo and Becky had left and the kids were in bed, Dale made smooth with Jude in the kitchen. "C'mon, hot mama," he whispered. Slid his hand around and got a handful of bottom.

"Dale Everett Banks. What in God's name are you doin'?"

Jude had a nice smile under a small nose and her large brown eyes had a sparkle he had not seen in many a night. "C'mon, baby." He reached for her tail end one more time and found another handful.

Now she giggled. A sweet sound he didn't hear enough. She turned to face him. Tried to keep a straight face, but couldn't. "You dirty old man, you." But she could not hide the grin that spread across her face.

He moved in for a kiss, a rare moment that did not come often enough for her. Their lips touched, and she felt his mustache stubble tickle her nose the way it always did. Banks worked his magic with his free hand, and his whispers sent warm feelings to places that had not felt heat in a long while.

"OK, take me upstairs, you stud," she said, and she turned and climbed up to the loft and waited. Banks pulled out his wad of chew and threw it in the sink. He rinsed his mouth and checked the locks on the doors. Turned off the lights and climbed the stairs and crawled in bed beside her.

Black night swallowed the day until the light was gone and a bedspread of darkness covered Goat Hill. Reverend Butch Pogue rocked back and forth with a slow rhythm that would either set you to sleep or keep you awake, and loose curtains swung in the musty air. Branches moved on the cottonwood outside the window, stained with film from a lifetime of heavy smoke and light cleaning.

Fall winds swooshed through the window behind him, and a broken wind chime crashed against the house. His chair rocked forward, and cobalt eyes radiated a malicious glow in the silhouette of darkness.

The rocking slowed as his dirty wife brought him a plate with two biscuits and a pile of burnt potatoes covered in onions.

The rocking stopped and the Reverend made a grumble in his throat. Hacked up a wad of slick yellow and turned his head and spat through the open window. Some phlegm chunks made it out, but most lay deposited on the ledge, where the sun from the east would find it come morning and bake it and sear it until it looked like crusted, scorched bird shit.

"What in the name of Almighty God is this?"

She pushed the round edge of the plate into his palm. "Take it."

"But there ain't no gravy, woman. I want gravy 'n' biscuits, not taters 'n' biscuits."

"You best take it," she said. "If you ain't gonna eat it, give it ta the boy."

Butch looked at the sturdy woman with shoulders too broad to hug and shook his head. Told her he'd eat it, but next time she best have gravy for those biscuits.

She let out what amounted to a snort, then stomped across the living room with heavy feet. Picked up where she'd left off in the kitchen. Before the old man started screaming for his fill.

Mama set the pig's head on the cutting board and peeled cold meat from the bone. She used her grandmother's knife and made soft easy sounds as shed peelings dropped into the blood-tarnished sink.

The head had thawed all morning but was still hard, the inside filled with ice.

Mama wrestled with it as best she could and cursed her husband for cutting through the muscle like he had and wasting good meat.

"That was Junior," Butch yelled. "Wasn't me that done it, woman. Now, you know better'n that. Y'know how I love pig brain."

The big woman dropped the knife into the sink and looked up through the window. "Now, whatta we got here?"

Butch Pogue watched a black-and-white movie on television without sound. They got one of three channels on a good day but never a clean picture without snow. He shoved a forkful of potatoes into his face and lines of thin ketchup ran in dribbles from his mouth and hurried over his stubbly gray chin.

Reverend Pogue was deeply involved in the program when Mama came back in the room. Told him to get his ass up, they had company.

He set his plate down fast on an end table filled with magazines and it slid onto the floor. He stood. "Comp'ny?"

His wife of many years went to shove him when she saw the mess he'd made, but Butch sidestepped her and drove an uppercut into one of her big sagging tits. She screamed and hit the floor. The Reverend told her pick up those biscuits. He didn't want them, but she was free to give what was left to the boy. He asked her if the boy had got that woodpile split. If there was company, there was work to be done.

Mama rolled onto her back. Her cheeks ripened as fresh blood pumped beneath the surface of her bulky jowls. She blew out a deep breath that brought tears to her eyes.

"You ought'n know better than try some shit like that on me, woman. We done been down this road before, and if my mind serves correct, you don't like where this road goes."

Mama pulled herself up and put her back to a tall stack of old newspapers. She held her tit with both hands and drew quick tight breaths in through her nose and out through her mouth. With every breath, her cheeks would puff and jiggle.

The preacher grabbed his rifle and walked to the front door like a man with purpose as headlights bounced up the rutted drive. Butch saw it was Jerry Dean bringing home the goods. Yelled out, "The prodigal son hath returned to his flock. Mercy me, we have been delivered. We have been blessed with this glorious bounty." He rambled on. "Thank you, Lord Jesus. Amen."

Jerry Dean shut the truck off and stepped out.

Butch Pogue approached with the rifle. Said, "We have been delivered, Brother."

He gave Jerry Dean a hug.

Jerry Dean stood solid like a big stump. Wide in the hips and thick in the waist and shoulders. He had a tank that hung over his belt, which gravity seemed to have gotten the better of.

The preacher was of similar build. Stocky with a great chest and an ample gut that rubbed hard against Jerry Dean's while Butch squeezed him and kissed his cheek.

"We have been delivered," the Reverend repeated.

Jerry Dean said, "Praise the Lord," uncomfortably, and Butch Pogue nodded.

The boy came around the corner with an ax.

Voices called his name in hushed whispers and warm breath washed over his face and neck. Sounds called to him in distant echoes. He saw his boys when they were young. Small faces and big eyes and fair hair untouched by a comb. They ran through tall yellow fields and waded through shallow creeks. He saw his wife, working in a flowerbed that had long ago sprouted weeds.

Olen Brandt saw his family in still pictures. Snapshots his mind forgot. The light was strong behind Arlene, it was evening, and in that moment her crown of golden curls became a halo.

"Look, Mom." There was Gil, so young. Such a beautiful boy. "Mama, look, watch." Gil shouted to her again, his kite taking to tall wind. Not just floating, *flying*, really flying. The wind pulled him hard across the yard.

She looked up, the halo illuminating her in a soft blonde glow.

"I wanna try, Gillie." Olen saw Gil's brother, Wade. So small and happy. *Before* prison. Before he was unrecognizable to the eyes of his father. Here, now, he was small and innocent and free.

Gil worked his kite and fought the wind, powerful gusts that jerked the string north, then south. Gil yelled with joy and beamed with pride. He'd saved for weeks to buy that kite.

"Here comes Dad," Wade yelled, and there was Olen. Pulling through the field on a Ford 8N, a tough old tractor that refused to die but had long since retired and become a yard ornament.

His family was right there. Waiting for him. All of them together now. Smiling and waving. He saw Sandy, too, sprinting after a rabbit and jumping a two-strand fence. Gliding smooth. Her coat sleek and fresh.

They called and waved. Said come home. Told him they loved him and missed him.

"Mr. Brandt, can you hear me, sir?"

His wife smiled and tears stained her cheeks and he wanted to kiss them. He reached for her, and her lips came together and said, "I love you." But then . . .

"Mr. Brandt, can you hear me? Mr. Brandt, come on, buddy, talk to me."

They were gone. Replaced by bright lights and strange voices.

"Olen, can you hear me? My name's Rayna. I'm a paramedic, and you're in my ambulance."

His eyes blinked and flickered, but the dark felt safe. Pulled him back.

"No . . . I don't . . ."

She rubbed a hard tool across his chest that smarted and his eyes popped open.

"There you are, Olen. Stay with me, buddy, OK?"

His head hurt like he'd been kicked by a mule.

"What happened to you? Do you remember?"

The light was bright, and he was cold.

"Where . . . are they?" he asked.

He was strapped to a bed, arms pinned to his side. Suddenly, everything shook and moved and the girl had to catch herself.

Rayna laughed. "Sorry, these damn roads are rough."

Olen came to, but struggled to make sense of what was happening. Was he dreaming? He thought about his family. Where was Sandy?

His throat was dry and it cracked when he tried to speak. "Where . . . are they?"

"I'm sorry, where's *who*, Mr. Brandt?"

"Where's my family?"

Rayna gave him a smile that showed her slight dimples and slipped a mask over his face. Said, "This'll help you breathe, Olen. Just relax. We're on our way to the hospital."

He felt clean air inside the mask, and it relaxed him. He let his eyes close. He wanted to let go of everything. Wanted to go back. Disappear into the darkness and wake up back in time. When the world was small and his family was waiting.

So young and strong and *alive*.

• • •

Banks met Hastings for breakfast at a Hardee's south of town, and the two exchanged greetings. "How's your head, boss?" Hastings asked.

Banks returned his grin. "Never you mind about my head, boy. How's that shoulder?"

"Shit. Good as new, Pops."

They'd started pitching horseshoes about ten o'clock the night before for what seemed like a good reason at the time but now neither could remember.

"Guess y'all made it home all right."

Hastings laughed. "Hell if I know, Dale. All I know's Mama woke my ass up in the driveway." He looked up at Dale. "Then I carried Mama up to the house, and it was on, baby."

Banks let out a great snort and shook his head. "Hell yeah, son. The old man got some last night, too."

Hastings laughed loudly.

"That's right, the old man's still got plenty of good fuckin' left in him, boy."

Hastings set his biscuit down on his plate and laughed until his face turned red.

They shared a few more hoots and chuckles, and Banks told exaggerated tales of past sexual conquests—some real, some imagined. Banks had been a real ladies' man in his day to hear him speak.

Hastings finished eating and told Banks he thought he'd

better go. Didn't think he could tolerate any more bullshit that early in the morning.

"Yeah, guess we better get a move on, youngster."

Before they could leave, Deputy Winkler walked in and nodded.

"Well, goddamn Winky, they'll let anybody in here."

Winkler said, "I was just about to say the same thing to y'all."

Banks and Hastings exchanged glances, each silently daring the other to bring up the motorcycle that outran Winkler.

Banks had the seniority and made his move.

"Yeah, we's just 'bout to roll out, Winky." He patted Winkler on the back and mentioned in a low voice he had an extra roll of duct tape out in the cruiser. "Case you used up all of yours on that light bar."

Winkler looked up, his face twisted into an ornery mess of frowns.

Hastings walked out before he lost it. Winkler looked at Banks and pointed.

"Fuck y'all, Dale. That son of a *bitch* was runnin' damn near two hun'ert mile an hour."

Banks grabbed his belly and staggered toward the door. "Two hundred, huh?"

Winkler followed, agitated though he'd seen it coming. Banks walked backward. Couldn't stop laughing.

"He *was* doin' over a hun'ert an' eighty for a *fact*, Dale."

Banks stopped at the door and put his hand on the butt of his Glock. "Don't make me shoot you, Wink."

They both grinned, and Winkler said, "Hundred and eighty, Dale. Black crotch rocket with a red helmet. You see that bastard, you shoot him."

Banks promised he would and left.

Later, Banks was doing paperwork at his desk when Sheriff Herb Feeler walked up and took a chair. Herb was an aging cowboy with grand ambitions to go places he never went. He was fifty-four and slim with a tight, square face that looked like country.

Herb wore a ten-gallon hat and pointy-toed boots. His top lip was covered by a Fu Manchu, his salt-and-pepper head shaved close. Herb chewed a toothpick like he was angry at all times. His gun belt was cocked below the waist, and he sported a Glock on his hip like a six-shooter. His brogue was southern and slow, his eyes small and precise, like he'd just as soon force you to draw as arrest you.

"How you doin', Dale?"

Banks held up a finger and finished reading the line he was on, then signed his name. He took off his reading glasses and said he was fine. Asked Herb how he'd been.

"Doin' OK, Dale. Doin' OK." He pointed to the paperwork. "That for the smurfing case you got there?"

Banks nodded. "Yes, sir."

Smurfing was the latest in illegal trends related to the drug trade. Tweakers would spend all day driving from one gas station to the next buying cold medicine, pseudoephedrine, the active ingredient in methamphetamine manufacturing. Street value was high. A hundred dollars a box or trade for crank. Most would trade for crank.

A month earlier, they'd busted a van full of college kids at the Fuel Mart. When they searched the van, they found hundreds of pills from gas stations and drugstores. The kids had saved all the receipts and made Banks's case easy.

"Listen, you know an old man named Olen Brandt?"

Suddenly, Banks could not swallow. It felt like someone had taken a baseball bat to his windpipe.

"Well, yeah I know him, Sheriff. He's got a farm out off Highway K—'tween Mount Sterling 'n' Swiss."

Herb nodded. "Yep, that's him."

Banks asked Sheriff Feeler why he'd brought him up. *Hoped it wasn't because he'd just stashed a duffel bag full of money in his barn loft.*

"Well, damndest thing, Dale. Somebody found the poor old sumbitch out there by that gravel pile last night. At the junction of K 'n' F."

Banks sat up in his chair. "Found him? What the hell you mean? He's dead?"

Herb threw his hands up. "No, no, he ain't dead. Not yet anyway. Tough old fart. A car come up on him 'n' his dog layin' out in the middle of the road last night."

"In the middle of the road? What in God's name you tellin' me, Herb?"

Herb shrugged. "Well, nobody knew what the hell to think at first. He liked ta got hit by a damn car, Dale. He's just layin' there. Out cold. Covered in blood from a head wound, his dog beside him. Somebody shot her dead."

"*What?*" Banks could not believe what he was hearing. "Hang on a minute here, Sheriff. Lemme get this straight. Olen Brandt was just layin' in the highway with his dog beside him?"

The sheriff shook his head and continued to shake it while Banks talked.

"What the hell happened to him? Who shot his dog?"

Sheriff Herb Feeler pulled a smoke loose from his pack and struck a wooden match against the zipper on his Wranglers.

Banks took a dip of snuff.

"Nobody knows what the hell happened, Dale. He sure as shit wasn't makin' any sense last night. But 'parently he's come 'round OK. Turns out he was haulin' a pretty big load of anhydrous yesterday evening and somebody jacked his truck."

Banks shook his head and spit into a Styrofoam cup. "Well, goddamn, Herb. Don't that beat all?"

"Never heard of that b'fore, but I guess it was bound to happen sooner or later."

"What'd they do to him?" Banks asked.

"Says he thinks he got outta the truck, but he can't remember a damn thing after that. Hell, Dale, I don't even know if he remembers steppin' outta the truck. But somebody musta flopped him a good one at some point."

"And the sumbitches shot his dog?"

"Killed her dead. Looked like she tried to protect him."

Banks stood and said he was going to talk to Olen. "I been deer huntin' on his place since I was knee-high to a grasshopper."

Herb said that was a good idea. Go and talk to the old man. See what he remembered.

Banks thought about the money he'd stashed at Olen's and hoped he hadn't gotten his friend involved. He made a list of suspects, and Olen's kin was at the very top. A nephew Banks knew ran with Jerry Dean.

If Banks was responsible for the old man's condition, he would never forgive himself.

He'd been hunting with Olen Brandt his whole life. Was a friend to Olen's boys, Wade and Gil. Grew up at the farm and spent many summers there. Before Gil died, before he and Wade grew old enough to drift apart, until Dale was a policeman and Wade was an outlaw stealing from river cabins and parked cars.

Banks had caught him once with stolen property and let him go. Told Wade he only got one pass. *Last chance to change your life*, he'd said. But Wade didn't listen.

A year later, he strong-armed a restaurant and fired a handgun. He did a good stretch in Algoa for that. Came out hard with a scar across his jaw. Said he'd changed. Started a tree-trimming business and turned his life around. But a few months later, he robbed a bait shop in a truck with his name painted on the door.

Dale and Olen remained close. They shared a passion for the outdoors and continued to hunt and fish. They hunted with compound bows and shotguns and muzzleloaders.

When Olen got too old to draw a bow, Banks bought him a

crossbow and a new wave of excitement filled the old man. They hunted whitetail and turkeys. Trapped coon. Then Arlene got sick and everything changed.

Wade got out of prison and worked construction. Did carpentry. But a nine-to-five job was not in the cards for Wade Brandt. One day, he and Duke McCray inhaled cans of whipped cream and robbed a gas station and a kid got shot.

Olen and Arlene could not sit through Wade's trial. A year later, she was dead, and Olen swore his son had killed her. When Arlene died, part of Olen Brandt went in the ground beside her, and a little piece of him died every day once she was gone.

Hermann Hospital was an old square building made of ancient red brick that sat a stone's throw north of old Highway 100. Banks went inside and found Olen Brandt staring out the window in a bed that was cranked up tall. He watched him through the doorway for a spell before he stepped inside. He loved that old man, and he was going to find those responsible. Banks had ideas about that. Hoped he was wrong, but doubted he was. He knew Olen had a nephew named Jackson Brandt just dumb enough to try this kind of thing.

His knuckles rapped hard on the inside of the doorframe, and Olen startled.

"Olen, it's me. Dale Banks."

Olen shook his head and motioned for him to come in. He looked old and tired. Like he was ready to give up and call it a life.

Banks reached down and set his hand on the old man's leg. "You OK, old-timer?"

Olen didn't understand why he was still alive. Tom Cuddy was gone. So was Sandy. So was everybody. Last night, in the space of a half hour, he'd lost the only two things in this world he had left.

Banks felt his pain. It resonated in the air like the frequency to a country station and Olen's life belted out a heartbreak song.

"I'm sorry, bud."

Olen nodded. Said he knew. If the old man cried, Banks would have to leave.

"Can I get you anything? Soda pop? Shot of whiskey?"

Olen said he just wanted to go home. He wasn't about to die in some damn hospital.

Banks gave him a grin. "You're not gonna die, old buddy. You're too dang ornery for that."

The old man tried to smile but couldn't.

"What do you know about last night, Olen? Who done this to you?"

He thought hard, but told Dale he did not know. He saw an old Chevy come out of the woods like the devil was after it, but that's the last thing he remembered.

"Old Chevy?" Banks asked. "Think you can describe it?"

Olen said it was dark, but he knew it was a Chevy. Something old. From the 1970s. "It was beat to hell on the outside."

Banks grinned and wrote. "Anything else?"

Olen said no. All he knew was that it didn't have a tailgate and the bed may have been blue. Or black. He said it happened fast. It was almost dark.

Banks told him he'd done good. That was a hell of a lot to remember. Especially considering the whack he took.

"Why'd they have to go 'n' shoot my dog?" Olen's eyes filled with a watery glaze. They bulged and strained, but they held. "I'da give 'em whatever it was they was after."

"Olen, I'm so sorry. I know you loved that dog."

"She was my wife's dog."

Banks thought about things he needed to do around the farm. Outside jobs he could do with the boy. He had to take his mind off the old man and his ache. "I'm gonna find these sumbitches, Olen. I promise you."

"You need to hang 'em when you do."

Banks said he'd do his best. He hoped they'd resist, and at that moment, he meant it more than he didn't.

"I wanna go home."

Banks said he'd already spoken with the doctor. Olen would be free to leave in the evening. "I'm gonna get back to work and see if I can't find these guys, OK? I'll make sure I'm back up here by five sharp to pick you up, all right?"

Olen thanked him and took his hand. His grip was strong.

"Where's she at?" he asked quietly.

"I went out there before I came here and made sure she's layin' under a shade tree. I'll go 'n' pick her up right now 'n' take her back to your place."

Olen said he was going, too.

"No, you need to wait. Let me do this for you. A man shouldn't hafta bury his own dog."

Olen let go and turned to look out the window. He watched a

cardinal zip around, jumping from branch to twig. "Thank you," he said.

Banks said he was honored to do it and felt his throat tighten up. He nodded. Told Olen he had work to do. He'd be back at five. Banks left the room and walked down the hall and felt a strong urge for a chew.

Hastings pulled up on the scene with caution and put his car in park. A domestic dispute between a felon and his wife at a trailer was the worst call he could imagine.

He opened the door and climbed out and patted his sidearm without thinking. Just making sure it was there. Because that was a good habit. The kind of habit that forms over time. Especially with a teacher like Banks to make sure.

Bo had been there before, at that mobile home. All of them had. Every deputy sheriff in Gasconade County had been to the trailer on Brockmeyer Road, and none of them volunteered to go back. It was a deputy's worst nightmare. Remote, and parked on a dead-end road, so they always knew you were coming.

Hastings stood beside his car and listened. The air smelled like burning trash. He thought about Banks. About what he would do if he were there. *He would pull the chew from his pocket and thunk the lid with his finger and open it and withdraw a pinch and a half and stick the wad behind his lip and push it down with his tongue.*

Bo Hastings reached for the walkie-talkie on his shoulder and held the mic.

"Gasconade Central, this is 109. Show me on location. Appears quiet at this time. I'm headed up to the front door."

"109, this is Gasconade Central. Let us know you need anything—case he gets outta hand."

"Gasconade Central, this is 109. Will do."

Hastings walked from the car and stood beside the driveway. What yard there was had once been dirt that became mud and was now sewage. There were planks of wood to step on and smaller patches of plywood that served as stepping stones. When Hastings, a solid kid with a broad back and wide shoulders, stepped on the first board, it sank a few inches and slid beneath his foot.

"Looks like we got us a sewer problem, Officer," Fish said, opening the door, trying to catch Hastings off guard, though he hadn't.

"Yeah, I thought I smelled shit," Hastings said. A response that would have made Banks proud.

Fish stepped onto the porch a little too quickly, and Hastings didn't like it. He halted and stood his ground and threw his left hand up. "No, sir. You stop right there." He flipped open his holster with his right hand.

Fish stopped. "Oh, big man, gotta gun. Well you cain't tell me what ta do in my own house."

Hastings's jaw flashed muscle. "Listen here, fella, you'll do whatever I tell ya. We gotta call from your wife. Said you beat her up. Now, where is she?"

Fish snorted and his upper body jumped around, though his feet were planted firmly. "Oh, tough talk. Like I'm supposed to be scared of you."

Hastings took a step forward and pulled the mace from his other holster. "Don't make me spray you, cuz I'm a pretty good shot."

Some cops missed, it happened—he'd seen it happen—but Hastings wouldn't miss. He practiced. Banks taught him to hit a coffee filter held to a tree branch with a clothespin.

"Where's your wife?" Hastings yelled for her. "Raylene?"

Fish moved quickly, angry and wired from crank. As he came at the deputy with all he had, Hastings fired a burst of mace, which thoroughly doused Fish's face, exactly where Hastings aimed.

Even with chemical in his eyes and nose and mouth, Fish charged him.

But Bo Hastings prepared for it. Threw a forearm into the face of his assailant and tried to sidestep him.

As they collided, Bo dropped the mace and spun toward Fish, grabbed him by the throat and held him. Fell to the ground and drove his knee into Fish's chest. Heard a rib snap like a dead branch.

Fish gasped and lost his wind, but Bo kept driving. Had to use momentum. Had to use everything he had until he could reach his gun. This was real life. It was happening, and the only thought in Hastings's mind was survival. He brought down a hard left and struck Fish in the jaw, and Fish's head snapped off the ground and he went limp.

The deputy heaved himself off and went to stand but lost his footing in the sewage. Fell on his back. Fought for his breath, and with a gut instinct for survival, thought of Kenny's wife, Raylene.

If domestic violence had taught him anything, it was that no matter how badly she'd been beaten, as soon as she saw handcuffs, *she*, the wife, or the girlfriend—bloody and swollen-faced and blackened-eyed—would recant her story. Because, in the end, despite all they'd been put through, they still did what they could to protect them.

So it would not surprise Hastings to look up and see her standing there with an ax or a shotgun. With tweakers high on dope, you never knew. Crank ruined people. Bo had seen it. Time and time again. Friends and neighbors and relatives. It took hold of them in ways they could not have imagined.

Half the county was on dope. Every week, without fail, arrests were made for possession of product, or precursors, or attempt to manufacture.

Hastings, buried in mud and shit, came to his knees and drew his weapon. Looked around with caution. Had to make sure Fisher's wife hadn't made a move.

He crawled toward Fish and removed his cuffs and hooked them around each wrist. Clicked them. Sat down and took a deep breath, then picked up his mace and shook the can and sprayed it in Kenny's face.

Fish screamed, as much as he could, and gagged. Tried to roll over but couldn't.

Hastings stood and spun around. Still waiting for an ax-wielding wife or a shotgun-brandishing next-of-kin to confront him.

Fish spit mud and mace from his mouth and threatened the kid.

"You're goin' to jail, you dumb son of a bitch."

Fish kicked blindly at Bo and cursed him.

Once he caught his breath and his heart rate slowed down—though it still had not returned to normal, probably wouldn't for a half hour—Hastings called Gasconade Central and requested an ambulance.

Then, because he deserved it, he kicked Fish in the ribs that weren't broken and sat down on the hood and waited.

Jackson Brandt woke up with a shotgun in his mouth.

Banks jammed the metal pipe between Jackson's teeth. "Wake up, cocksucker."

Jackson's eyes were white moons covered in red veins. He could not speak, though he tried.

"Don't talk, just listen."

Jackson shook his head up and down.

"You're a dog turd on the bottom of my work boot, boy. You ain't nothin' but trash to me. You understand that? Cuz it's real important to me you understand that."

Jackson tried to stay calm, but the tube was in his mouth. He tried to talk, and the cop shoved the barrel deep into the back of his throat. It felt like he was dying.

"You understand what I'm sayin'?"

Jackson nodded. His eyes watered. Banks worked the stock back and forth until Jackson puked into the barrel and it ran back down in his mouth.

"I am a God-fearin' man, Jackson Brandt. Yes, I am. And because I'm a God-fearin' man, I know it is my sworn duty to eliminate shit bags like you and make this world a better place for my kids."

Jackson did his best to say no and shook his head.

"I'm gonna ask you a question—and if you lie to me, I'll blow your throat out through the back of your head."

Jackson screamed into the gun barrel and cold puke bubbles seeped from the barrel and ran down his cheeks into his ears.

"I know what you're thinkin', boy. I'm a cop, so I won't do it. But lemme tell you somethin', son. Take a good look at this gun. This is *your* gun."

Jackson tried to turn his head. His eyes looked to his left, to the corner, where his 20-gauge was supposed to be.

"You lie to me and you're just another white trash bum who ate a shotgun."

Jackson tried to speak, but he was choking. He begged the deputy with his eyes.

"Don't you lie to me."

Jackson could not breathe. He swore with his nods and his gestures.

Banks removed the shotgun and words began to spew from Jackson's mouth along with a burst of vomit. "It was Jerry Dean that done it. It was Jerry Dean, man. I swear. If you's gonna shoot somebody, shoot him."

"Was Jerry Dean done what?"

And with that, Jackson was alarmed. Did his best to proceed with caution.

Was there a cop in his room because of Fish, or because of Jerry Dean? Or maybe it was the prison guard who got busted—*not that he should know about him*, but sometimes Jackson heard things. Some things he remembered; some things he forgot. But he had not survived the game for as long as he had by talking to police and answering questions.

Banks asked again. "What about Jerry Dean?"

"It . . . it was Jerry Dean Skaggs took my uncle's truck and shot his dog, man. . . . It was him. Honest. I didn't want no part of it, man, I swear."

Jackson sat up, tried to catch his breath. He pointed to his bottom lip, the wound from Jerry Dean's fist still mending. "He done this, too."

Banks reached down and slammed Jackson in the mouth with a straight right and his lip busted open.

Jackson screamed, "You sumbitch, why'd you hit me? Ah, goddamn, that hurts!"

"I ain't even asked you a question yet, dipshit."

Jackson rolled onto his side. "If that ain't what you wanna know, then why the hell're you here?"

"I was just gonna ask about that ridin' mower you got for sale out there in your mama's yard." Banks threw the shotgun at Jackson and bounced the stock off his head. "Get up, you piece of shit."

"Ouch! You . . . this is bullshit, man. This is police brutality. I know my rights."

"You don't know shit."

"You pulled a gun on me, man. You coulda *kilt* me."

"The gun ain't even loaded, you dummy."

Jackson moaned and cried, and Banks flipped the cap on his holster.

"But this gun here, this one *is* loaded, fucknuts, and I'll drop you where you lay and say you pulled on me. Different scenario, same result. Now get your ass outside. You're comin' with me."

Banks drove gravel roads to the farm with Olen's nephew in the backseat and his dog in the trunk. He told Sheriff Feeler he was taking the rest of the day off to tend to Sandy's disposal and feed Olen's cattle.

Sheriff Feeler said that was a good idea.

"Why I gotta ride back here?"

"Keep talkin' and you'll switch places with the dog."

"Man, that's fucked up. I know he loved that old dog."

"Then why'd you do it for? You robbed your own kin."

Jackson didn't have an answer. He wanted crank and that was the easiest way. "I didn't think he's gonna get hurt, man. You gotta believe me."

Banks spit brown tobacco juice into a Mountain Dew bottle, then returned it to the cup holder. "You're about as worthless as titties on a catfish."

"Man, I'm scared of Jerry Dean. Fucker's crazy, man. He said it'd be easy. My uncle had insurance."

"You make me wanna puke."

"He said my uncle'd make good money from it. Said I'd make a lil' money, too. I just went along with it."

"Where's the tanks?"

Jackson went silent for the first time since the gun was in his mouth.

Banks looked into the rearview mirror, and their eyes connected. "The tanks?"

"Jerry Dean took 'em."

"No shit. Just know I'm only askin' once."

"What're you gonna do this time, shoot me in the backseat?"

"No. I'll pull over and shoot you—'n' bury you in the same hole as the dog."

They turned onto another gravel road and followed the branch to the right, along a country mile of rolling hills and sagging fence.

"Tanks?" Banks said. "Last time."

"Am I under arrest?"

"I ain't decided yet."

Jackson knew you could not trust cops, but either way he went put him in a pickle. "If I tell you what I know 'n' whatnot, you gonna let me go?"

"If you tell me what I wanna know, I'm gonna let you live."

Jackson knew Banks from previous occasions and numerous arrests. If he were going to shoot him or arrest him, he'd have already done it. "What if I make you a deal?"

"I'm listening."

"Jerry Dean's got some pot plants growin' on the Gasconade. He's got a bunch o'—"

Banks cut him off. "I don't give a damn 'bout no pot plants. I want them tanks."

"Well, what's in it for me if I tell?"

"How about not getting shot?"

"If you was gonna shoot me, you'd've done it already."

Banks shook his head. Told Jackson he was wrong. He wasn't shooting him until he buried the dog; he'd need him for another hour. That hole wasn't gonna dig itself.

Banks watched Jackson dig a hole and sweat while he sat in the air-conditioning and talked on the phone. When Jackson finished digging to a depth that satisfied Banks, he popped the trunk and the smell of dead hide blew out.

Jackson held his breath, reached down, and scooped her up. He groaned. Said, "Oh, shit, she's heavy."

"Walk her to the hole and set her down *gently*."

Jackson did as he was told.

"Now fill it."

Once Jackson finished, Banks pulled his handcuffs out and told him to turn around. "Put your hands behind your back, shit bird. You know the routine."

"Aw, c'mon, man. I dug the hole. What more you want from me?"

Banks slapped the cuffs on tight and spun Jackson around and pushed him up against the car.

"What now?" Jackson asked. "C'mon, man. What're you gonna do with me?"

"You got any dope on you, boy?"

Jackson was appalled. "Hell no. Course not."

Banks reached down to Jackson's pocket and felt the glass pipe.

"What's this? Feels awful hard to me, and I'm pretty sure it ain't your little peter."

"That ain't mine."

Banks said, "Uh-huh. Course it ain't."

Jackson had enough. "My lawyer's gonna sue the shit outta you, pork. When he's through with you, you'll be workin' the cash register at Fuel Mart."

Banks shook his head slowly. Said, "You 'spect me to believe a man with a five-dollar truck livin' in a seven-dollar trailer can afford a lawyer?"

"That ain't my truck. It's Jerry Dean's."

"Well, that's nice to know, asshole. But it don't matter. Jerry Dean's name don't come up on the tag. And bein's possession's nine-tenths of the law and all . . ."

"Oh, no, that ain't mine. Jerry Dean *loves* that truck. He made me drive it home."

Banks kicked Jackson's feet apart and told him to spread 'em. "I ain't gonna get jabbed with a needle if I reach in here, am I?"

Jackson was beginning to fall apart. He told Banks he could go to hell. "Wait till Jerry Dean gets through with y'all."

Banks pulled a glass pipe from Jackson's pocket and held it to his nose. "Smells like a possum's asshole. How can you boys smoke this shit?"

Jackson kept quiet. Wondered if Banks heard what he'd said.

The deputy searched his other pockets. He found four dollars and a small torch, but no meth.

"Where's the Bob White?" Banks asked.

Jackson kept a silent tongue, so Banks drove an elbow into his back and applied pressure. "Where's the dope?"

Jackson squirmed and told Banks he was out of crank.

Banks spun him around. "I'm takin' you in, peckerwood."

"For what?"

"Well, where do we begin? Grand theft auto, assault with a deadly weapon, animal cruelty, possession of drug paraphernalia. But mostly just for bein' an asshole."

"Stop," Jackson yelled. "Just lemme go, man. I done whatchya asked."

Banks bore holes into Jackson's face with his thousand-yard stare.

"C'mon, Sheriff, you know I ain't done this. This ain't me, man. It was all Jerry Dean."

Banks pulled his pepper spray and held it to Jackson's face.

"No!" Jackson screamed and turned away. "That shit burns like the dickens, man. It still burns from the last time I got sprayed."

Banks grabbed him and shoved him out of the way so he could open the door.

"Jerry Dean knows y'all took his money."

That got Banks's attention, and he froze.

"Oh, boy," Jackson said. "Look at that face, man. Somebody's been a bad cop."

Banks felt like he'd just been run over by a semi.

"It's true, then," Jackson said.

"What money? What're you talkin' 'bout, convict?"

Jackson had a used car salesman grin that revealed a face full of meth mouth, bits and pieces of teeth in assorted states of decay.

"You *did* do it. For real. You really are bat-shit crazy, Sheriff."

"First of all, I ain't the damn sheriff, I'm a deputy. Second of all, asshole, I ain't the one out robbin' my own kin and killin' their dogs. So don't try 'n' confuse your own white-trash existence with mine."

"You don't understand, man. You need me. We both want the same thing."

"Yeah, what's that?"

"See Jerry Dean go back to Algoa."

Banks was in a tight spot, and he worked hard to bully up a poker face.

"Bullshit," Banks said. "He's your dope connection."

"Yeah, Sheriff. I mean, Deputy, he is. But you don't understand, man. I want *off* the shit, I do. It's just too dang hard. And him comin' 'round beatin' on me and pushin' that shit in my face don't help none."

Jackson was desperate, but Banks saw honesty in his words. "Just what exactly are you tryin' to sell me?"

"I ain't tryin' ta sell you nothin'—but I'm gonna end up dead or in prison myself if he don't go back. And that ain't what I want, man."

Banks removed his Skoal and thunked the lid. "Well, that's the smartest thing you said all day."

"That's because I know it's true. I want off that shit. I got plans. I'm openin' a small engine shop. I can work on lawn mowers all day long, man."

Banks never considered himself a good liar, but he held his own when he asked Jackson what money he was talking about.

Jackson put his head down and looked at the dirt.

"You know, the fifty-two g's one of y'all took." Jackson looked up at the deputy. "Man, I'm tellin' ya, you don't know what y'all've gotten yourselves into."

Banks shook his head and lied poorly. "I ain't got no idea what you're talkin' 'bout, convict. What would a low-life shit bum like Jerry Dean be doin' with that much cash?"

"It ain't all his. He splits it up with his guys, you know?"

"His partners?"

"Yep."

"And who're these partners?"

"C'mon, man, I cain't say."

"You best tell me." Banks gave the mace a quick shake.

"All I know's one of 'em's a cop. They supply dope to the prison. But you didn't hear none of this from me."

Banks was genuinely stunned. "You're tellin' me there's a cop in on this?"

"You mean you really don't know?"

Banks didn't answer. He had never considered the idea, nor had he expected it.

"Well, yeah." Jackson shrugged and turned his palms up. "There's a cop in on this."

"A cop . . ." Banks shook his head in disbelief. He couldn't finish.

"Yeah. Damn, man. There's a cop involved. *Now* you know."

Banks was dumbfounded. "I can't believe a cop'd be stupid enough to get in cahoots with you idiots."

Jackson threw his arms up dramatically. "Why's that so damn

hard to believe? You cops ain't no better'n the rest of us. Hell, y'all're worse. You think that badge is a right to steal."

Banks spit brown juice in the weeds. They stood at the edge of the lower forty. Under a pecan tree where Sandy had spent many summers. It was her favorite spot to nap in the shade while Olen worked the land.

Banks looked at the fresh mound of dirt. Made more spit. Told Jackson to be straight with him. His future depended on it.

"Listen, all I know's what he mumbled last night. He was madder'n I ever seen him. But more'n that . . . he was worried."

"Go on," Banks said.

"We's smokin' that shit, you know, gettin' ready for my uncle—but I was hopin' he wouldn't come, I was." Jackson looked nervous. Tried to swallow but had a hard time of it. "I need water, mister."

Banks just stared at him.

"So anyway," Jackson said, "Jerry Dean come by the house, and he's madder'n a wet cat. He starts shakin' me down, man. Like he always does. Takes the rest of *my* dope I got stashed and starts smokin' it up. Says how you stole his money."

"How *who* stole his money?"

"I dunno. I thought it was you. Thought that was why you showed up at my place."

Banks shook his head. "Well, you thought wrong."

He felt a cold wave of nausea run through him and spit juice on Jackson's boot. He drove him back to his mama's trailer and told him he would see him soon. It was in his best interest, Banks said, not to mention this to Jerry Dean.

Jackson swore he wouldn't.

Banks spent the rest of the afternoon at the Brandt farm. He fed Olen's cows and chickens. Saw to it that they had water. By a quarter of five, he arrived at the hospital. Olen was waiting out front. He met Banks at the curb, before he could park.

"You OK, Olen?"

"Just get me the hell outta here."

"Sure thing, buddy. They *did* release you, right? You didn't just sneak out, did you?"

Olen looked at Banks. "What if I did?"

Banks fought a grin. "Well, then I guess I'm helpin' you escape."

Olen nodded. "You damn right. Hell with them doctors."

Banks had a good laugh and encouraged Olen to relax. "You hungry over there, hoss?" Banks asked. "I know that hospital food ain't exactly home cookin'."

Olen said he was starving. The food at the hospital was tasteless, and his iced tea had no flavor.

"What sounds good, partner? How 'bout a Silver Dollar?"

Olen said that'd be fine. He hadn't had a Silver Dollar burger in . . . He tried to recall but wasn't able.

"We've had many a burger there, haven't we, old buddy?"

Olen looked back in time, nodded. "Lots of burgers, that's right."

The Silver Dollar was a metal shed nailed to a dirt parking lot on the side of Highway 19—a straight shot across from the Swiss processing plant. It had a reputation for the biggest cheeseburgers in a hundred miles. Burgers so monstrous they were served on kaiser buns and held together by wooden spears. They came with a steak knife to saw through the meat. The two had been eating there for years.

While they waited for the food, they chatted with the regulars who crowded their table to hear from Olen Brandt. Seemed the whole county knew what those tweakers done to his dog, and they were angry.

Olen told what he remembered. The death of Tom Cuddy. A wild turkey. A Chevy made of rust. He didn't tell anyone he'd seen his family, or how badly he'd wanted to join them.

A short, round man with two chins who was stuffed into a pair of bib overalls said, "What color was that truck?"

Olen cocked his head and squinted. "It was"—he paused—"it was yella 'n' white, I think. With a dark bed, I think. I know it didn't have no gate on the tail end."

The fat man shook his head. "I think I know that truck."

Banks winced.

"Yeah, that's that Skaggs boy from out yonder at Helmig Ferry."

Suddenly, the room was filled with deep breaths being taken and hushed conversations. But no one was surprised.

"What're y'all doin' 'bout that, Dale?" someone asked.

Banks set his coffee cup down on the counter. Said they were looking into it.

"Well, we can't be havin' farmers out there gettin' carjacked," said the fat man.

The others agreed.

Banks nodded his head. Said that was true. "I'm pretty sure we'll catch these turds. Just give us a few days to work the case."

"What's to work?" asked the fat man. "That Skaggs boy's lower than a copperhead's peter." He nodded to the two ladies present. "Pardon my French, ladies—but you know what I mean, Dale. That Jerry Dean's the same one shot that bald eagle a few years back."

That got everyone talking and sounds of great disgust radiated from the crowd.

Banks knew it was true. Jerry Dean damn near outran Sheriff Feeler one night back when Herb had been a deputy. It was the first year he'd run for office. They were on a straight stretch outside Morrison. Jerry Dean was weaving back and forth across the white line when Herb ran up on him.

Herb followed. Gave him plenty of room. When the swerving got erratic, he lit him up. But Jerry Dean had other plans. He made a run for it, and did a fine job of running until he swerved to miss a ten-point buck and slid his truck into a wheat field.

The cruiser Herb was driving was the one and only car with a video camera so the episode already had the making of a country legend.

The chase ended as Jerry Dean stumbled drunkenly from his truck into the path of Herb's cruiser and got hit by the bumper and thrown on the hood, his drunken face up close against the windshield.

When Herb searched the truck, he found a dead bald eagle riding shotgun with a wing blown off. Jerry Dean swore he'd found it on the road. Said he planned to glue it back on and turn him loose.

The arrest made big news. Because Herb arrested Jerry Dean with a bald eagle *and* because he hit him with his car. In an election year, that was gold. Herb Feeler was in like Flynn. He traded his cruiser for the sheriff's truck. Then he strutted into office in a Stetson with a Fu Manchu and took the first of many steps he hoped would lead to the governor's mansion.

They rode in silence to the Brandt farm. When they pulled in Olen's driveway, Banks said he'd fed the livestock and tended the chickens.

"I set a dozen or so eggs on the porch. Inside that sun hat on your readin' chair."

Olen thanked him. "You didn't have to do that, Dale. I don't know how to repay you."

"Aw, horseshit, Olen. Now, you don't owe me a dang thing, and you know it. I've spent my life out here. Givin' a friend a hand in return's the least I can do."

Olen wanted to fill the air with tears, but instead he laughed. He laughed at the thought of Banks on the Allis-Chalmers, in his uniform. Laughed at the thought of Banks in the chicken house.

He looked over, saw Banks had a stern look on his face.

"Before you even ask, yes, that damn rooster tried to attack me, Olen. Thought I'd have to mace him."

Olen threw his head back and let out a sharp hoot.

They each drank a Coke and watched the fading sun go down from the old man's porch, where it fell behind the barn in a pink death and burned into a purple ball that became night.

"You gonna be OK out here by yourself, old-timer?"

Olen took a deep breath. Face pale and tight.

Banks gave the old man's shoulder a firm squeeze. Bid him good evening and promised to call in the morning.

Olen said, "OK."

He thanked Banks again for all he'd done. When Banks drove away into the darkness, and when the last hint of red taillight began to fade, Olen finally realized he was alone, and he did his best not to cry.

Jerry Dean spent the night on Goat Hill and made a promise to himself never to return. He and the preacher smoked fresh product from a tall glass hookah that pulled the crank through fruit-flavored water that pooled in the bottom of a clear oversized bowl.

It was a two-man operation. One man would light the bowl with a butane torch while the other man hit the mouthpiece. Gravity pulled the smoke down into the water, and they sucked wisps of strawberry meth up the glass neck.

Butch Pogue soaked chemicals in coffee filters during the production of crank. When the batch was complete, he immersed the potent filters in fruit punch, then drank the punch over ice in a plastic shaker. He called it Jehovah's Blood, and it propelled them into the night like rocket fuel—though the conversations it brought forth both mesmerized and terrified Jerry Dean.

The Reverend proclaimed himself a prophet. Said he'd taken a new wife. She was a young and beautiful soul who filled them with hope and enriched their lives with promise. The prophet said they kept her in the basement.

Jerry Dean was aghast when he looked at the old house, and his mind was invaded with unimaginable horrors at the thought of what might be in that basement.

Jerry Dean had only seen one of the Reverend's wives. The big wife with the dirt face. She hadn't left the hill in twenty years, not even when Butch did his stretch.

But Mama was a big-boned stocky *bulk* of a woman who knew how to work a knife. Jerry Dean was convinced she could take care of herself. She could live off the land in the Reverend's absence as well as any man.

The cultivator and the preacher had smoked speed all night. Until the Jehovah's Blood got the best of the Reverend, and he began to rant. It was a spiritual awakening that washed over him and cleansed Butch Pogue in a wave of Holy Gratitude.

Jerry Dean was getting out there about as far as he cared to go. His mind was warping and bending. But he was trapped. His place was on the hill until the Reverend said it wasn't.

Butch stood on his soapbox and beckoned his family as he pounded his chest and gave thanks to the sun. He cast out the demons that slept in his mind and admonished the devils that swam in his heart. Screamed, "We have all been forgiven," over and over again.

Jerry Dean turned and saw them stumble from the farmhouse. The big woman and her slow son and her husband's new wife—her long brown hair combed to look straight, curls semi-restrained but ungovernable.

Butch Pogue tore off his shirt and flung it to the ground. "We do this for you, Oh Great One," he screamed, voice dry and breaking. "I offer you this sacrifice."

He yelled for Junior to bring him a pig.

Butch Pogue Junior was a man in body, but his mind was dawdling and unhurried. He'd never seen a movie or been to school. Jerry Dean wasn't sure if he'd ever been down the mountain, and it would not surprise him to any degree if he hadn't.

"C'mon, boy. Bring me a pig," the Prophet demanded.

Junior did as he was told. He nodded his head and shuffled his feet and disappeared into the woods for a longer period of time than Jerry Dean was able to account for—yet he was in awe of the strange ritual he found himself a part of. A bizarre ceremony with a perverted lunatic, a retarded son, and a stolen bride.

Junior returned. Pulled a swine with a rope onto the mound of elevated earth where his father stood and tied the pig to a stump.

Butch held his arms to the sky, and his eyes rolled back in his head until the razor-sharp cobalt was a memory and they showed solid white.

The preacher began preaching and appealing to the highest of callings.

Jerry Dean felt chills, and the sun hid behind clouds and the sky turned gray. Butch Pogue preached in the shadows, the sound of his voice hoarse and failing.

When Jerry Dean looked at the girl, he felt a stir under his belt buckle. Her skin was fresh and new, the color of eggshells. Like it had not felt the sun's heat in months.

She begged for help with every shiver.

Butch kicked his sermon into overdrive and pulled a machete from his makeshift pulpit. He looked at his son and his wives and nodded with approval.

He looked at Jerry Dean and his mouth was moving, but Jerry Dean did not know the words. The Reverend spoke in tongues. In a language of gibberish squalling and cackles.

His new wife squinted when the sun reappeared. Jerry Dean was drawn to her. Wondered how she would look without that ball gag in her mouth. Lips stretched thin and pink. Eyes hollow and gray and dead. Like the sky above them. Like everything inside her heart had been destroyed and replaced by cardboard.

But somewhere inside was a spark of life. If only he could find it.

"Brother," the Reverend commanded.

Butch handed Jerry Dean the knife and began a rant that was heard by all and understood by none.

Butch squeezed Jerry Dean's palm around the handle. Held his head with his free hand. Their eyes locked onto each other and their foreheads touched. The Reverend said, "Kill that swine, Brother Jerry."

Brother Jerry took the machete.

As he walked to the mound, Jerry Dean looked into Mama's soulless face and her eyes grew impossibly wide, her facial bones twisted and contorted. She chomped her sharp teeth, but they weren't teeth, they were elongated ivory razors.

Mama whispered, "I'm gonna eat you soon."

Jerry Dean swung the blade into the pig's neck, and blood sprayed the yard in a fine mist. The pig jumped and bucked and squealed, and Jerry Dean pounded that swine with the blade until it was dead and Butch had fresh blood across his face.

"Can you feel that?" he asked Jerry Dean. "Can you feel that, Brother?"

Jerry Dean watched the pig fall to the ground, and its short fat legs kicked and its hooves pushed up grass and it bled out in the dirt.

Butch took Jerry Dean by the arms and whispered in his ear, "Can you feel that, Jerry Dean?"

Jerry Dean said he could, and Butch said, "Praise the Lord."

The air smelled like death as Butch and his wives danced without music.

Banks watched the sun creep over the forest of oak trees and a crack of light broke through the night and grew longer and wider and ate the black like a fungus until the darkness was gone and there was light and it was day.

He dumped a cup of cold coffee in the grass. Banks had spent another restless night thinking of the money. He thought about Olen, too. About Jackson Brandt, and all the new problems taking the money had created. Banks thought about his options and remembered the conversation they'd had. Maybe somehow, someway, Banks could use him.

If there *was* a cop collecting money, Jerry Dean would tell him—and whoever that cop was would know Banks was dirty. Though Banks did not think of it that way. Banks was a family man. He knew he should give the money back. They would survive without it. Giving it back was the right thing to do.

But now he couldn't. Or if he could, he didn't know how. He did not want to involve Hastings. Banks could not have that hanging over his head. The kid had enough to worry about. Ten years back, his old man had driven his patrol car into a minivan full of carolers. It was Christmas. They were going to see the lights.

Bill Hastings was drunk and everyone else died.

A week later, he got in a bar fight, then jumped off a bridge into the Missouri River. He drowned before his case went to trial.

Banks knew that was a lot for a young man to swallow. He'd do his best to protect Bo.

Banks spent the better part of the morning with the Lake Area Narcotics Enforcement Group. Helped them serve a search warrant at a property on Highway P.

It was a ranch-style home made of rock and tan brick with a big spread of land and a manicured yard. Banks could not believe how bad things had gotten. It wasn't just the shit bums who got addicted to the pipe. It was blue-collar people who rolled their sleeves up and went to work every day. It was a white-collar banker, like this guy. Caught up in a world he did not understand.

Banks sat on the hood of his patrol car and studied a ripened cornfield. Watched the pale sky with thick patches of broken cloud drift above the rows of brawny stalks.

The banker had a meth lab in his barn, but he said it wasn't his. He let a guy cook on the weekends, and he kept some of the product. Thought he'd never get caught.

"Nobody does, asshole," Banks said. He shook his head while another deputy took the banker into custody.

Banks was tired of seeing his town fall apart. The banker was a member of the chamber of commerce, a pillar of the community. Every damn day someone new went to jail for crank, and it gnawed at Banks like a splinter under his toenail.

Winkler walked up and asked him what he knew.

Banks pointed to the cornfield. "I know some sumbitch needs to combine that corn."

"Sure 'nuff," Winkler said. "It is late in the season."

"Uh-huh."

The wind swirled dust, and Winkler looked up at the clouds. "Sure could use rain."

"Ain't that the truth," Banks said. "It's drier than a popcorn fart."

Winkler shrugged. Chewed on his lip. Banks contemplated a fresh pinch of Skoal.

"Hell of a thing right there, Dale. That's the same sumbitch turned me down on a loan for that Gator Boat I wanted."

Banks laughed and spit. "That right?"

"Oh, it sure is."

Banks bent over and dug the spent wad of chew from the bottom of his mouth with his tongue and let it fall in the dirt. "I reckon you don't feel too sorry for him, then."

"Not at all."

"Well, I don't blame you none there, Winky. I remember you's madder'n hell."

Winkler shook his head. "I'm still mad."

Around noon, Banks put in a call to Olen Brandt and got nervous when he didn't answer. He decided he'd pay the old man a visit, but a car wreck happened first and he got sidetracked. A history teacher had rear-ended an eighteen-wheeler in front of the local Walmart.

It didn't sound good.

Banks responded quickly to the scene. Only to be beaten by Dan Marnier, the editor of the town newspaper.

"You must have a police scanner jammed up your ass, Marnier," Banks said.

Marnier was always first on every scene and never missed an opportunity to film dead bodies. A teacher, grandparents, kids. It didn't matter. Marnier took their pictures, and people hated him for it.

"One of these days, that'll be you in a wrecked car and I'll be takin' *your* picture."

Marnier smirked but kept his mouth shut. He was a small-town boy with big-city dreams who had never left the county. Taking pictures of dead bodies was his way of contributing.

The teacher—Jim Hanson—was huge in the gut, bigger than Banks. The steering wheel of the Ford Ranger had crushed him. Smashed his rib cage into his heart and shoved his guts out through his asshole.

Banks checked for a pulse, but it was over for Mr. Hanson.

Banks thought about Bo.

Jim Hanson had been his football coach and mentor. He'd spent a lot of time with the kid in school. Did his best to fill the void created by Bill Hastings's departure.

Banks cringed at the thought of Bo pulling up at the scene, which, any minute, he would surely do.

A few minutes later, first responders arrived. Followed by the volunteer fire department. Earl Lee sprang from his Mustang in khaki pants and a fireman's hat and started barking orders.

Banks stepped back to direct traffic while Marnier got in for the close-ups.

Deputy Winkler pulled up and climbed out of his car and walked toward Banks. "That ain't Mr. Hanson, is it, Dale?"

"Was."

"Oh, gosh dammit. Shit. Fuck."

Winky threw the bottle of Dr Pepper he'd been holding on the ground.

"Sorry 'bout that, Wink. I know y'all was close."

"Yeah, Dale, but not as close as him 'n' Bo."

When Winkler saw Marnier snapping pictures, he blew a gasket—but Banks had anticipated such a reaction. Grabbed his arm. "You don't wanna do this."

But Winkler said he did and made his move. Banks let him go and did his best to direct traffic.

"You put that camera away right now, Marnier, you son of a bitch."

"I'm just doin' my job."

"Well, you gonna be doin' it with a broken jaw you don't put that camera down."

They argued and Winkler yelled, and finally, after much swearing and spitting and threatening, Marnier limped away. Like a dog that just had its teeth kicked in by a steel-toed boot.

Winkler, red-faced and sweating, walked back to Banks and nodded.

"Feel better?"

Winkler said he did.

Then Hastings pulled up and sat in his car. He stepped into the sun with his head hung low. Walked toward the both of them. Winkler walked toward him.

"Is that . . . ?"

"Yeah, I'm afraid so, Bo. Poor Mr. Hanson."

Hastings stopped. Lowered his head.

Winkler said, "Bo, you go on back to the ranch. We got this."

Banks agreed. Told him, "Get."

"Go on, now," Winkler said. He grabbed Hastings by the shoulders. Spun him around, pointed him toward his car. "We're on this, bud."

Hastings nodded. Walked back to the cruiser. He climbed in and put on his seat belt and started the car and pulled onto the road.

• • •

When Fish got out of jail, he was alone. His family had abandoned him. And since the bank had repossessed their trailer, he had nothing left to show for his miserable life but a handful of cinder blocks and a twelve-by-sixty outline on a patch of hot dirt. *But at least he had his shed*, and then they came and took that, too. Took his tools and his supplies and a half-ounce of crank that was hidden in his Igloo cooler—a half-ounce of crank he had to get back if he wanted to save his trailer. It was not too late. Long as there was air in his lungs, he would fight.

His wife took the boys and moved in with her mom, then left the kids with her mom and moved in with his cousin. Turns out she'd been seeing him for a year, and Fish should have seen that coming. But he was too busy making crank, which was his way of providing.

After he'd accused her of fucking his cousin, an accusation she'd denied, Fish had kicked her and punched her and loosened her teeth from the gums.

On the floor, bleeding and crying, she'd called 911. Begged him to stop—but he'd driven his fists into her stomach anyway. Then the kid had shown up, they'd fought, and Fish had been falsely arrested. Unjustly imprisoned.

And that was the last time he'd seen Raylene.

Now his wife and kids were gone. And, looking back toward previous days, the warning signs had been there all along. If only he'd taken the time to see them.

But all of it was *his* fault, to hear her speak. Because he'd never had a good job or been to college or got a degree, though she did not complain when he gave her the money he earned from the crank he made—crank she claimed not to know about. But she knew. Women in her position always did but pretended not to.

And so Fish found himself lost and homeless and broke. Living in his pickup truck, trying to survive. He drove by the Bay Bank, slowly. Second gear at an idle. The old truck pushing smoke through a rusted exhaust pipe.

He'd watched the bank for years. Planning for the day when he'd have just enough balls to rob it. Now, after everything in his life was gone, he had found them.

It would not be hard. The bank had two rooms, and the town of Bay was small. A few dozen people on a two-lane road—half of them beyond their golden years. The building itself was as old as the people, built in the 1800s and owned by a woman who should have retired but chose to hang on.

Hanging on was all she knew. Taking people's money was what she did. Taking mobile homes from family men gave her a reason to go on living.

But taking the shed that served as his meth lab had been the final straw.

He could see it in the parking lot, beside his family's trailer. The back had been damaged during transport, and a window was missing. Old and broken and sad. Pink insulation hung from its belly like the guts of a wounded beast.

Fish would come back late that night with bolt cutters and

clip her lock off the door, retake what was rightfully his. He would snort line after line till the sun came up—and then it was *her* time to pay. He would charge inside the bank with his shotgun and reclaim what belonged to him.

Or maybe he wouldn't, though he ought to. *But his main focus was the crank* and what he knew he could do with it. There were a handful of people on standby who would take it off his hands. Give him back everything he'd lost a hundred dollars at a time.

He shifted gears and nudged the gas. The truck rumbled up the small hill and down the other side and disappeared past Fowler's creek.

Fish took back roads to a clearing in Olen Brandt's field. He limped his pickup through a shallow ditch and drove to the river. Parked beneath a sycamore tree and twisted a doobie and lit it. Watched the sun bake golden ripples where the water hit the shallow spots.

There was a 12-gauge beside him and a handgun behind the seat.

Fish pulled a hit from the joint. He coughed and thought. There were a pair of gloves on the floorboard and a ski mask. Fourteen rounds of buckshot and a clip for the .45.

He hung his head out the window and spat. Saw his face in the side mirror and froze. Looked at himself. When did he get so old? There was a scar across his chin that curved at the end and was made by a two-by-four. They'd been leveling their trailer when he'd stomped it in half with his boot to make a shim. When he did, the wood broke and jumped up and drove a nail in his jaw. Split him open.

Fish bled for a day and thought he'd never recover. But that was because he would pick. He would pull the scab off while it was fresh and caress the pink scar with his finger.

His entire life was one long scar.

Fish sat back in the cab and drew another hit from the joint and watched a family float down the river. There was a man and two kids in a johnboat with a 35-horsepower Merc. He saw a beer cooler and some fishing poles. Memories being made they would never forget.

In a different life, that was *him* and *his* two kids, before he had failed them. Or him with his sister and dad, before his sister was cut to shreds and his old man turned to drink. Before his mom worked two jobs until the cancer ate her bones to powder and she died a pile of skin.

Fish watched them float and cast and talk. Watched them love one another in a way he had not been loved. It was a love that you read about in books or saw on TV—Dad baited Junior's hook, and he *laughed* when it hit the bank. He didn't drag his knuckles across Junior's cheek like Big Fish would have done.

No, this dad was perfect. He grinned and shook his head and ran his fingers through Junior's hair.

Fish pulled a deep hit in his lungs and held it and bumped the key and started the truck. He had to leave before he cut them down. The tires spun in the dirt as he turned and left the river. Relaxing his lungs, he set the joint in the ashtray and shifted gears. He had a few hours to kill. He thought about the shotgun and the ski mask and the crank. He thought about the banker and the cousin and the payback.

For the first time in a long time, Fish began to smile.

Butch Pogue Junior spent the afternoon taking Olen Brandt's truck apart. He removed both doors and gutted the inside and placed the seat up against the wall to use as a chair. He thought about his daddy's new wife. Thought about how strange she looked with that ball gag. Daddy warned her to keep quiet, but she didn't listen. Daddy showed her.

But Junior was a good boy. He listened. When his daddy said to take that truck apart, Junior did as he was told. They could use the truck on the farm. Daddy promised to let him drive.

The Reverend walked into the shed with pig guts in his chest hair. Asked the boy if he'd seen Brother Jerry.

The group had spread out after the sermon. Junior went to the shed, and Mama took Daddy's new wife out back for a shower in the garden hose.

The Reverend couldn't find Jerry Dean.

Jerry Dean Skaggs was taken with the Reverend's bride. He hid behind the woodpile and watched Mama spray her off. Looked on in stark horror as Mama washed the soap from the girl's privates with want in her eye.

"Brother Jerry."

Jerry Dean jumped at the sound of the Reverend's voice and took to fast walking toward the dog pen.

When Reverend Pogue came from the barn, he was covered in pig's blood with a shaker full of Jesus Juice and a rusty machete. "Jerry Dean," he called scratchily.

His voice was gone. Throat raw and cracked like an old chunk of concrete.

The beasts in the kennel stirred dirt and dust and barked with ferocity. They gnashed their teeth as steel-braided cords and knots of sinew bulged under tight skin, their fur clipped short, the mass of brawny muscles popping and flexing and threatening to destroy.

"Where you been, boy?"

Jerry Dean was going a hundred miles an hour inside his head. The Reverend was insane. He would chop him into short pieces and toss them in the woodstove if he knew what he had done. He would not take kindly to Jerry Dean spying on his wife.

A red pitbull mix jumped at the fence. Jerry Dean saw it had one brown eye but the other was gone. It had a dash of strawberry-blond on its muzzle, and its chest was thick and wide.

"Sweet Wine," the Reverend said.

"What's that, Butch?"

"That's Wine."

The Reverend reached his hand into the fence, and Wine stopped barking. The dog nudged the Reverend's palm and snorted, then barked. And then the other dogs fought for the right to lick their master's hand.

The Reverend looked unhinged as he stood in the shadows. Told Brother Jerry it was time for him to go.

"We feed these animals meat."

He turned and walked back to the barn.

The Reverend gave Jerry Dean a ride to the bottom of Goat Hill in a rust-bucket truck that didn't seem fit to make the trip. They crossed the creek and water came up through holes in the floor-board and Jerry Dean had to lift his boots.

They drove the back roads until they found more back roads. Dust thick and red. The Reverend dropped Jerry Dean off a mile from his cousin Ronnie's. Said there wasn't no need for anybody's kin to see.

Jerry Dean agreed readily. He wanted out of that truck.

He walked the long mile to his cousin's in the sun and thought about his situation. He also had a partner to think about—Bazooka Kincaid—who had a derby car to pay for, and he would not let Jerry Dean forget it. The Firecracker 5000 was coming up, and Bazooka Kincaid aimed to enter.

Jerry Dean would have to see him soon. Then his thoughts shifted to the girl, the Reverend's wife. Jerry Dean could not stop seeing her in his mind.

When he got to the trailer, there was commotion out front that he could see from a distance. Darlene had a laundry basket filled with clothes on the hood of a Pontiac Bonneville. She was screaming at Ronnie. Threatening to leave.

Her brother, Ray, was there, too. He was also screaming.

The fighting stopped when Jerry Dean walked up the driveway.

"Well, ain't this just the icing on the cake, Ronnie Lee? If it ain't your dumbass cousin. Same one tried to rape me."

"You wish," Jerry Dean said.

"You grabbed my titty and you know it."

Jerry Dean brushed past them without words. He was tired. His body hurt, and his eyes burned from being awake. Said he was goin' to bed.

Darlene shot Ronnie a look. "He ain't sleepin' in my bed."

Ronnie said, "Now, you just wait a minute, Jerry Dean—"

"Fuck you!" Jerry Dean gave Ronnie the finger. "It ain't her bed no more if she's leavin'."

Jerry Dean had to get sleep before his eyes caught fire. He also gave Ray the finger.

Ray laughed. "Don't bring me into this, bud. But, hey, now that you's here, we gotta talk."

"Later."

"You know Wade Brandt's 'bout to get out, don't ya?"

Jerry Dean grunted and swore. "I know this. Been lookin' ta tell you the same thing."

"Well, what're y'all gonna do about it?"

"We'll talk later."

"It cain't wait. I need a little o' that Bob White, Jerry Dean. Them jailbirds is hot for it."

"It's cookin'."

Jerry Dean threw the door open, and the room smelled like trash.

He walked to the back and took off his boots and lay down on the bed and slept.

He awoke the next day, and the house was quiet. He thought about the dreams he had. The ones he could remember. Dreams about the girl in the basement.

Jerry Dean shivered and felt strange in ways he was unaccustomed.

He sat up and stretched. Put on his boots and tied them and opened the door and left the room. Ronnie sat at the kitchen table with a roll of aluminum foil in his hand. His other hand held a Bic. There was sweat on his forehead and drool in his chin hair.

"Damn, it's quiet in here. A man could get used to this."

His cousin looked up. Nodded. Said he had bad news. That bitch Darlene was gone.

"She is?" Jerry Dean shrugged. "Well, good on you then, man. She's a bitch if ever there was one. How you put up with that cunt bag long as you did, I'll never know."

Ronnie shrugged again. He picked up a scrap of tin foil off the table and passed it to his cousin. "Want a hit?"

Jerry Dean said, "You betchya," and picked up the foil and held it to the light. He found the pile and tilted his wrist and struck the Bic. The powder smoldered. He inhaled the smoke through the plastic tube and held it and exhaled. A dense cloud that held the weight of chemicals hung in the air.

He lit the pile again and moved the tube across the foil—capturing every last wisp of smoke—and handed the foil back to his cousin.

"So where'd that old lady o' yours run off to this time?"

"She's stayin' with her brother."

"Uh-huh. That'll last until tomorrow."

Ronnie shook his head. "I know but"—he paused—"I think she might be seein' someone. Caught her writin' a letter the other day. I asked her about it, 'n' she folded it up quick 'n' stuffed it 'tween her tits."

He looked at Jerry Dean. "I'm afraid she might leave."

Jerry Dean grinned. "Well, you best enjoy this while ya can. Go out 'n' get you a whore for the night."

"Shit," Ronnie said. "Darlene'd cut my nuts off."

"She'll never know."

"Yes, she will. She'll know."

Jerry Dean thought about that. Said Ronnie may be right.

They polished off another foily and Ronnie drove him to Jackson Brandt's trailer.

Bazooka Kincaid was a redheaded, short, stout fireball of a man with a beer keg chest and shoulders that stretched the length of a shovel handle. He swung the ax into a chunk of fence post. The sun beat down on him, and he swung the ax, again and again, until the cedar post was a pile of pink splinters in the dirt.

"You best finish up here, then move along," Ned said.

Ned Barstow was a small, thin waste of space with pale skin that looked slick with sweat. He had Bazooka splitting old fence posts into small hand-wood for the potbelly stove in his office.

Bazooka swung the ax and sank the blade deep into a rotten stump that crumbled in dead black chunks.

"Load up that truck, Kincaid. Then get. Come back on Monday." Ned picked at his nose with a pinky. "Best be on time, 'n' don't plan on leavin' here none too early. We got us a hell of an order lined up."

Bazooka Kincaid was a fifty-gallon drum filled with dynamite. His arms were like thick limbs of an oak tree, fat and hard at the shoulder, and they worked down to wrists the size of steel pipe that grew into wide, bulky hands strong enough to crush a man.

"You hear me, Kincaid?" Ned's sharp voice was a splinter in Bazooka's eardrum and a high pitch north of where it should be.

Bazooka nodded. Said he heard just fine. He'd be back to work on Monday. But Ned Barstow ignored him and walked back to his office and slammed the door.

A cool wind gushed in the bottoms and was felt by all. Trees blew and branches shook and leaves fell to the ground and crunched under Bazooka's feet.

He walked to his truck, ax slung over his shoulder, eyebrows pushed tight, almost touching, save for a wrinkle that separated one from the other, a dirty pudge of skin like a break between two cornrows.

His truck, which had been ready for the junkyard when he bought it, hobbled from Barstow's turkey farm as the sun hid behind clouds. Summer had come and gone; fall would be brief. He felt winter in the air. Tonight he would build a fire if he found the strength, though more than likely he would not.

Bazooka trudged through ruts and potholes, and the dashboard rattled and shook.

He slowed the truck to a roll and crawled through a washed-out section of county road that was a deep gouge across the earth, carved into the gravel and red dust.

He bounced through to the other side. Turned on Pigg Hollow and drove two miles of tattered weather-beaten path that grew to a trail and led to an old single-wide mobile home somebody had unhooked from the truck and dropped in the dirt. A mobile home somebody long before him resided in but now looked fit to burn.

There was a window missing in front and no curtains to sway in the wind. Leaves blew in the hole and covered the floor. Bazooka had no running water inside, and his well pump coughed and sputtered a brown stream that smelled like eggs.

He drank from a five-gallon gas can he'd bought new and kept for intake and showered with rainwater collected by the green and yellow buckets on his roof.

Bazooka Kincaid poured himself onto the couch and opened a beer and drank from the can, paused long enough to catch his breath, then drank until he finished it and tossed the can on a pile of empty cans.

By the third can, he felt something.

Bazooka reached beneath the couch and fingered for a green tin. He found it. Pulled it up onto his belly and opened it. There were a handful of joints inside. He selected one and jammed it in his mouth and lit it and drew small puffs and coughed.

Bazooka Kincaid was on fire inside. It was harvest time, and he was restless. He trusted Jerry Dean about as far he could throw a piano. But he needed money.

He pulled a hit deep into his lungs and held his breath. Thought about nothing in that moment. It was a dull gray moment without color. He held it as long as he could, and when his chest felt like it would burst, he released the breath and his cheeks swooshed, his lungs burned. He coughed and hacked up a mouthful of phlegm. Swallowed it and gagged and took another hit. His body ached from chopping wood, and the more wood he'd chopped, the more he thought about chopping up Ned Barstow.

Bazooka turned on his side and set the joint in the ashtray on the floor. The hours of this day were numbered. He wrapped himself in a blanket and closed his eyes and went to sleep.

Jackson Brandt was sleeping when Jerry Dean started hollering his name and pounding on the door. "Wake up, you shit dog."

Jackson rolled over and stood up. There was a small bag of crank on his nightstand. He picked it up and looked for a place to hide it, but could not find one.

He set it back down and placed a CD on top of it.

He took a deep breath and opened the door. Jerry Dean was standing on his front porch. When the door opened, he pushed his way in and the first words to escape his lips were the same first words that always did. "Got any shit?"

Before Jackson could say no, Jerry Dean moved him out of the way. Stepped into the bedroom.

"Now, get out, you fucker. I ain't got nothin'."

Jerry Dean walked to the nightstand, the closest thing within arm's reach from the bed. He looked over at Jackson, who looked nervous.

Jerry Dean picked up the CD and grinned.

"Well, how nice. Lookie what we got here, Mr. Jackson Fuck-face. You's holdin' out on me, brother."

Jackson walked toward Jerry Dean as he picked up the baggie.

"Mind if I lay me one out?" he asked.

"As a matter of fact, I do."

"Don't worry. I'll lay one out for you, too, boss."

Jackson stomped down the hall. He took a piss and splashed water on his face. He thought about the shotgun. Thought about shooting Jerry Dean, then calling Banks. He thought hard about it.

Jackson walked back into his bedroom to find Jerry Dean had scratched out two lines of crank and snorted them both. He handed the CD case to Jackson. "Sorry, dude. I waited, but I didn't know where you'd run off to."

"I was takin' a piss!"

Jerry Dean shrugged. "Well, sorry, man. I looked for you, I did."

Jackson grabbed the bag of crank and folded it up and tied the top of the bag into a knot and stuffed it into the tiny pocket above the right-side pocket of his Levi's.

"What do you want?"

Jerry Dean turned his head to the side. "Whatchya mean, what I want?"

His pupils were black ink stains that seemed to grow and expand as he spoke.

Jackson shrugged.

"Well, I come to get my truck, numbnuts. That ain't a problem for you, is it?"

"It ain't a problem at all."

Jackson dug the keychain out of his other pocket and tossed it to Jerry Dean.

"Your mama's lookin' real good today, dude."

Jackson frowned.

"Seriously, Jackhole, how big a gal is she? Four hun'ert fifty? Five hun'ert pounds?"

"That'd be 'bout my guess."

"Boy, I'd love to get hold o' somethin' like that," Jerry Dean said. "I'd pound the hell outta that big ass. I'd get up in there and knock somethin' loose."

Jackson said nothing.

"Hey," Jerry Dean said. "Wonder when the last time was your mama had a hard rod stuck up her butthole?" He grabbed himself in a most revolting fashion.

Jackson took hold of the shotgun and raised it to Jerry Dean's chest and blasted him onto the bed and into the wall. What lead missed Jerry Dean's face made holes in the wood, and beams of light shone through and illuminated dust motes that mixed with the blood spray.

"Hey, dickhole, *you still with me?*"

Jerry Dean picked up a beer can that had been used as an ashtray and hit Jackson Brandt in the nuts. Jackson jumped and the can hit the floor. Ashes and bent cigarettes spilled on the carpet.

Jackson looked down at Jerry Dean sitting on his bed. *Alive*. No blood on the wall. No holes. The shotgun was still in the corner.

Jerry Dean stood. Told Jackson he looked like a zombie. "You need to get some sleep, dude. *That* I know."

Jackson nodded. Jerry Dean was not shot dead. He was right there, though Jackson was not sure if he felt relief or disappointment.

"How's about a bump for the road, old buddy?"

Jackson shook his head no.

Jerry Dean said that was fine. The Reverend had a batch cooking. Hell, it was off gassing by now. They'd be well supplied before long.

"That oughta give you somethin' to look forward to," Jerry Dean said.

Jackson said it did.

"Don't worry 'bout none o' this. 'Fore long, this shit'll be all worked out, you'll see."

"What about the cop?"

"Yeah. What about that fucker?"

"Well, what about the money? How y'all plan on gettin' it back?"

Jerry Dean thought about it. Said, "You oughta not concern yourself with that, sport."

Jackson looked nervous. "But this shit's about ta go sideways on us, Jerry Dean."

"Jackson, you are correct. But trust me here. I got plans for that cop, all kinda plans. You'll see."

"Yeah, but you cain't be killin' no cop, Jerry Dean."

Jerry Dean took a step back inside the trailer, but Jackson held his ground.

"Listen here, you cornholin', sister-fuckin' . . . I don't even know what. We's all 'bout ta find ourselves in a world of shit, you hear me? A world of shit, and somethin's got ta be done." He gut-pushed Jackson, made him take a step back. "I got me a business ta run, Jackson. And we don't do somethin' now 'bout this sitchuation, then we's all fucked, and it'll all be over but the cryin'."

Jackson hemmed and hawed. "Well, what if you just deal him in?"

Jerry Dean gritted his teeth. Started yelling. "Oh, that's a great idea. Then we got *two* greedy pigs we gotta deal with. 'Sides, this guy ain't likely ta take that deal anyhow I don't reckon."

Jackson shrugged his shoulders and bit the scab on his lip.

"We's all in the middle o' this here bind, and I'm hear ta tell ya it cain't end well for all of us."

"Why not?"

"Cuz it cain't."

Jerry Dean turned and walked back outside and climbed in his truck and started the engine and backed out of the driveway.

Fish drove to a hunting cabin out at Brown Shanty and parked his truck beneath a hackberry tree with a smiley face painted on the side that faced the river. It was a visual landmark that told boaters they were close to Held's Island.

He entered the cabin with a key that hung above the doorframe, to the right; it was far out of reach unless you knew where to find it, which he did, having seen Buck Ramsey use it when they'd cooked meth last fall. The key's location had been insignificant at the time—but a guy like Fish had taken note of a thing like that. Never knew when an empty hideout by the river might come in handy.

Fish stepped inside with a Walmart bag that held his belongings and set the bag on the table. Removed a bottle of water and walked to the bathroom and prepared for the night to come. Found a sink and a used razor and shaved his face clean of scruff.

Decided he should rest.

Fish lay on a worn-out couch in the corner and finished the joint and slept until late evening. And he dreamed of Raylene. Dreamed he'd carried her body in his arms for a long journey. Into the deep woods.

He'd climbed the face of a rock-strewn bluff and held her above his head, then slammed her to the ground and broke her back across the boulders.

In the dream, she wore a red dress and she screamed when her backbones shattered.

Fish was aroused when he opened his eyes, but angry. Angry at the thought of being alone, but aroused at the thought of killing her.

He stood and dressed and stumbled in the darkness until he stood before the fireplace. Reached up to the mantel and found a candle. Once it was lit, he held it in front of him and walked toward the bathroom and pissed in the sink. Set the candle on the shelf and searched his reflection in the shadows. The mirror was dirty. He rubbed his crotch and bit his lip.

Fish adjusted the candle so he could see, then reached in his pocket and found *it*—the fix he'd been waiting for. The whore he had resisted for ten thousand nights.

An electric sensation gripped him as he held the needle. It was a powerful moment.

He looked down, arms in gooseflesh, thoughts of poison kisses in his veins.

Fish clutched the needle between his teeth and opened and closed his hands. Slowed his breathing and watched strips of lean muscle twist under thin skin.

His reflection: black and flamed and nonexistent.

Fish repositioned the candle, then pulled the baggie from his pocket and held it toward the flame and removed the twisty tie and dropped it on the floor and opened the bottle of water he set on the sink before his nap and poured just a drop in the lid and mixed in some crank and removed the syringe from between his teeth and took off the lid and stirred it and worked the plunger a time or two, then pushed it forward and purged the air from the tube and drew up a little meth inside the needle and held it up to his neck and pinched the skin with his free hand and slid the tip of the needle into the thin blue vein that ran across his collar bone.

And then he was free. He closed his eyes and felt the world detonate. It was warm and black and slow. Both terrifying and beautiful.

It was everything he'd ever felt, all at once, and at that moment, no one else on earth had ever felt as good as him. There was an explosion inside his body that melted everything within him and charred his guts and his soul and whatever heart he had left. Numbness excavated a once shallow burrow to a now gaping depth.

Fish felt his body against the wall, behind him, slide to the worn linoleum. Feet straightforward in the darkness. Above him, high on the shelf: the candle. So small. Lonesome and burning, its flame flickering, caught in the mirror's translucent glow. The light, so far away, like he was sitting on top of the earth and that flame was the sun. Its distance was immeasurable, yet close enough to dream of touching.

Every part of his body was hot and bendy, almost liquid. Like he would melt and run down the air vent in the floor like hot candle wax and coat the dusted patch of concrete below the crawl space in a warm human stain.

Fish left Brown Shanty in darkness. It was cold with the window down. He felt the crank inside his veins, loving him. Warm velvet that peppered his soul like a whirlwind of bug bites. His skin was more aware of sensation than it had ever been. Damp hairs on his arms felt like melting ice penetrating his flesh, cutting to the bone.

It was as though he was floating above the truck, looking down and seeing the truck, while he was also inside the truck, behind the wheel, looking up—seeing him see himself watching himself driving.

Fish could feel a trail of fire climb up his spine and spread across his back with deep, scorching burns. It gave him beautiful thoughts and sensations with clarity he had never known.

But he would need another shot, and soon; he was going to lose this quick.

However long it had been since the last shot he didn't know. But clearly it had been too long. He breathed. His fingers opened and closed and relaxed their grip on the wheel. His shirt was very wet with sweat, and he could smell his stench, suddenly and completely.

He had to do this before he lost his nerve.

It was well past midnight when Fish parked on Hog Trough Road and walked a mile to the trailer. He admired the setup Early had. The kind of place a man like Fish could only dream of. There was real siding and a shingled roof. Skylights in the kitchen.

There was a part of him that did not blame her. But a part of him that did.

He walked up and stood beside the AC unit and looked through the window. Saw his cousin on the couch, hand buried in his filthy boxers.

How that wife of his could let him inside her Fish would never know.

He walked to the back door and reached for the knob and turned it. When it clicked, Fish slowed his breathing and pushed the door open and heavy boots stomped down the hall.

Early looked up as Fish racked the gun.

"Holy shit, no—"

Fish shot him as he stood, and the window blew out behind him. His cousin fell to the couch, and it rocked. Stuffing filled the air where the body landed.

Early rolled off the cushion, then fell to the floor.

Fish, scared and nervous, sweating profusely, turned and walked to the bedroom and kicked open the door. It was dark. There were loud, sharp screams in the blackness.

Fish reached for the light switch because he wanted her to see him. Wanted her to know that he was the one who shot his cousin, her lover, and know that he was the one who was about to shoot her.

"No, Kenny," she screamed as the lights went on. Like she had known it was him already. Like she had dreamed he was coming to see her.

She sat flat against the headboard, sleep in her eyes and hair full of tangles. A child beside her, his son. Screaming, eyes open. He called out for his dad.

Fish lowered the shotgun and turned from the room and ran—out the back door, down the steps. Inside, his wife was screaming—calling out his name.

Fear raced through his body, pounding his ears. Fish stopped and leaned against the rough bark of a shag hickory and puked.

He was shaking as he put the gun on safety. He stood and breathed deeply and ran to his truck in the blackness. So late it was early, with no light above him. A sky without stars.

Another second and he would have shot his son.

• • •

Fish talked to himself as he drove. Windows up, radio off. He thought about what he had done, and what he hadn't. Fish closed his eyes and watched that fat bastard tumble to the floor—dumb look on his face with chunks of fat blown from his chest, dead with a hard-on in drawers with a skid mark.

Fish passed the bank and took Route W, turned right. Drove a mile and crossed a bridge and turned on Little Bay Road. Parked his truck behind a gravel pile.

Fish grabbed his bolt cutters and his ski mask and his shotgun and walked through the woods. To the bank. Through a dry creek bed that had not seen rain in months. He climbed a white picket fence that ran for two miles and cost more than his trailer.

He walked slowly, like a man unconcerned with traffic.

Fish got to the bank and circled around it. His shed waited where the repo man left it. He had pushed it off his rollback truck and let it drop onto the gravel.

Fish snapped the chain and stepped inside—but everything was missing: his tools and his workbench and the vise he'd mounted to it; his grinders and his welder *and the cooler where he kept his crank*—worth two thousand dollars—enough to get their trailer back.

Enough to get Raylene back since he hadn't killed her.

Fish stumbled in the early light and tripped over debris in a futile attempt to find it. His Igloo cooler was the only thing in the world that mattered. Fish dropped to the floor and cried with his head in his hands. Sweated and swore. Laid down on the floor and slept.

It was the sounds of life that awoke him. Birds chirped on a telephone wire above the shed. A passing car blew its horn. There was a swing set in motion at the house next door and the voices of children playing.

Fish came to his feet and pissed in the corner. There were tools here and there. A yellow newspaper and old batteries and two broken fishing poles. A light beam pushed through the window and stirred dust in the air.

On the floor, he saw the ax that belonged to his dad. Thirty years old, with a chipped blade, a missing chunk from the handle where the old man hit a stump.

Fish picked up the ax and studied it. He thought about his life and his wife and his dead cousin. About the options he had left, which were few.

There were memories in his life that never existed, with a family that could have been. But everything went wrong. His sister died and his mother died and his dad became a monster.

"What in the hell're you doin' in here? What in God's name, Kenny Fisher?"

She startled Fish and he jumped. Ms. Vivian Dixie: late seventies, white hair, never married. She owned the bank and the store, and she worked six days out of seven.

She had taken his trailer and his shed and his wife and his sons.

Fish stood, trembling. The shed smelling like warm piss behind him.

"You got no right to this stuff—*it belongs to the bank*—and I let that boy with the tow truck take what he wanted. That was his price for haulin' it."

She looked down at the lock that was dangling. "My God, Kenny Fisher, you're trespassin'. I done called the law. . . . Now you owe me a new lock."

Fish stepped forward and swung the ax. Used his shoulders and swung hard and sank the blade between her eyes.

Her face popped like a decaying log and she dropped to her knees, life exiting her body like a *swoosh* of foul wind.

He released the ax and she fell on her back—legs bent beneath her, face pushed in like a rotten pumpkin, ax jutting like a growth.

Fish stood motionless, looked down at his hands. Calloused and dirty and blood splattered. Then he looked at her. So small and so broken. A lifeless carcass, nothing more. It was grotesque—her body—the way it had contorted. Her age-spotted hand, reaching. Bent fingers. Like she tried to crawl out of her skin.

He stood there for the longest time and thought, watching the blood flow. It poured from her white hair and ran toward the lowest wall of the unleveled shed.

When Vivian Dixie had called the police, Scott Winkler was on duty. Ten minutes from Bay, he held his foot to the floor. If Kenny Fisher had come for his shed, then there'd be hell to pay. He was out of his mind with rage, and surely high on crank.

Winkler called for backup. Thought things might get tough. The bank had uprooted the trailer just as soon as Fish went to jail. It was a coordinated effort with the police, and they had kept Fish for as long as they could.

When Ms. Dixie saw her chance, she took it. Struck while the iron was hot. C & K Towing hooked up to the trailer and winched the shed onto a rollback.

Fish came home to a dead-end road littered with bags of trash. His worldly possessions were a truck with four bald tires and a pair of old Wranglers stuffed in a Walmart bag.

Winkler drove fast and the engine screamed, but he kept the sirens quiet. Didn't want Fish to hear him coming and give himself away.

Deputy Winkler pulled into the lot and put the car in park. Sat there. He did not see Fish or Ms. Dixie or anything out of place. He opened the door and spun sideways and climbed out of the car.

When Fish heard gravel crunch under tires, the anger that never quite left him returned, overpowered him. As he stomped from the shed, Winkler climbed from his car and closed the door.

Fish raised the shotgun and squeezed the trigger but nothing happened.

Winkler, caught off guard, yelled and dove to the ground.

Fish, more surprised than anything, had never been more embarrassed. It stunned him to realize that after shooting his cousin he'd forgotten to cock the 12-gauge.

Winkler, flat on his belly, with a clear view of legs, fired four rounds into both cowboy boots and put Fish to the ground.

Winkler stood quickly and watched Fish. Rolling in the dirt and screaming.

He thought about shooting him again. Wanted to and still might.

Fish, climbing to his knees, slowly, and in considerable pain, looked down and saw one foot spun backward and both boots filled with meat.

"Put the gun down, you motherfucker," Winkler yelled.

Fish saw only black and white. His whole body burned. *His feet were gone.*

"It's over, Fisher. Now come on, man. Put down that gun."

Fish was sweating and bleeding, but he had just enough strength to rack the 12-gauge and place it under his chin. Reach down with his thumb and push the trigger and take a shotgun blast to the face.

Winkler stood by the car in shock. Took a few steps forward and stopped.

Fish had blown the top of his skull off, and there were parts of it on the shed. The blast had removed his face and tore his head in half. There was nothing left but red bones and teeth and skin that looked like pizza once you scraped the meat off.

Winkler walked backward toward the car and collapsed in the seat and used his radio to call in. Told Gasconade County through code words what just happened. He couldn't believe he'd almost died, and he couldn't believe Fish killed himself. *He'd just done it.*

"Hurry up," he told them.

"Sit tight," they said.

Everyone was coming.

The air was cold when Bazooka opened his eyes. It was daylight. Mid-morning. Sun poured through the window and bathed him in warmth.

He rolled over. Tried to sleep, but couldn't. Wide awake. He may as well go to town for supplies. Stop by the turkey farm and fill his gas can with water.

He walked unsteadily out the back door onto cinder-block steps and pissed into a patch of poison ivy. Already thinking of the tin and the weed, he stumbled inside and took a seat on the couch and fired up a doobie. Looked on in wonder at the plants drying inside his trailer, obsessed with potential profit and the derby car it would provide.

It had been a long road to the Firecracker 5000. Many years he had bought and saved and toiled—collecting cars and various parts: engines and radiators and transmissions—and now the time was upon him. There was a Lincoln Town Car beside his trailer with a roll cage, five-point harness, and a power plant under the hood—soon to be rebuilt by the best mechanic in the county.

With the new engine and his hunger and his raw determination, the potential for success was apparent and the possibilities for his future were endless.

The road to town was rough. Pigg Hollow was a buffet of

potholes in a variety of depth and size. The front end of the truck lunged through a furrow and the windshield popped.

When he got to the bottom of Hog Trough Road, he met Jerry Dean in his beat-up Chevrolet.

Bazooka pulled up next to the truck and turned off his engine.

"Was just on my way to see you," Jerry Dean said. "We got us a serious problem."

He told Bazooka what had happened. One of two cops had taken the money. Or maybe both cops had taken the money and split the jackpot. Either way, fifty-two grand was all they had. It was a green light to cook and sell and transport dope without being pulled over.

It was also *his* share of the profit. What Bazooka had been waiting for. The money for the 460 Big Block that would destroy its way to victory.

Bazooka punched the windshield of his truck and spider-webbed the glass.

"Calm down, Red."

"We gotta get that money, J.D. I gotta derby car ta build for the big spring smashup. Hell, it's less than six months away—and this bein' the Firecracker 5000 we're talkin' about. I been waitin' all year for that one. Hell, I been waitin' a lot longer'n that."

"Yeah, Red. I know, *I know*."

He looked up the hill. "And that old trailer I got's just fallin' apart. Got my whole future tied up with this deal."

"Uh-huh. Mine too, Red. And don't forget my trailer ain't no better'n yours."

Bazooka Kincaid stared at Jerry Dean. Asked what they should do. "This is some bad goddamn timing, you know that?"

"Surely, I do."

"Not to mention we got more crops to pull. Sumbitch, it's gonna frost next week—hell, it dropped down in the forties last night."

"I know man, it's gettin' close. And once they frost, they're done."

Bazooka got loud and ejected a burst of spit out the window with his words. "So what in God's name you suggest we do? Cuz you do not seem too worried."

Jerry Dean shook his head like he understood. "I got this figured out. It's a hell of a plan, trust me."

"What's that?"

Jerry Dean asked Bazooka Kincaid if he had any weed.

"Up yonder."

"Let's go 'n' get high. We'll talk about it."

Bazooka Kincaid said OK and turned his truck around and followed Jerry Dean up the hill.

They sat at a picnic table made of rotten wood and Jerry Dean laid out a plan for his associate. "Now, Red, you're 'bout the only man in this world I trust . . . and you know that."

Bazooka lit a doobie and pulled a few quick hits and passed it.

"Cuz I got some shit to tell you. I been thinkin' 'bout this for a while now."

"What's that?"

"Just chew on this for a minute, will ya? See . . . you think about it, *we're* the ones goin' through all this trouble—truck-jackin' people 'n' whatnot. Shit, Red, that's the biggest risk right there. We need to be at the other end of this deal."

"What d'you mean?"

"I mean, *we're* the ones need to be up top on that hill."

Bazooka thought about that and watched Jerry Dean babysit the joint. "We need to be on what hill?" he asked. "Are you *high*? I'll be goddamned I step one foot on that hill. I'd rather light my cock on fire."

Jerry Dean held the joint between his shit-stained fingers, and Bazooka watched the paper burn down while smoke drifted from the end. Bazooka didn't like that, good weed they had worked so hard for being wasted. He snatched the joint from Jerry Dean's clutch. "Goddamn, Bogart. Hand it back."

Jerry Dean caught himself staring at the ground and shook his head. Told himself snap out of it. "Anyways, I been thinkin' here, Red. That Reverend's crazier than a coon dog with two peters. I cain't say as I trust that sumbitch no more at all. Hell, yesterday I thought he might just as soon kill me as drive me back ta town."

Bazooka said he understood. "That Reverend's nutty as fuck, but damn if he ain't the best cook I ever seen."

"And that there's no lie, the man *is* good, Red. *That* I will give him. But he's fucked up in ways I cain't describe." Jerry Dean tapped the side of his head with a finger.

"I know," Bazooka said. "You don't have to tell me. I did time with the man."

"I reckon you did," Jerry Dean said. "How could I forget?"

Bazooka Kincaid had drawn time in Algoa a good ways back. He'd gotten out near the same time Jerry Dean went in. Bazooka had done four years for armed robbery. He and Wade Brandt were robbing Cracker Barrel restaurants and using the proceeds to finance a derby car. They were planning for the Firecracker 5000. An annual event Bazooka had spent the better part of ten years trying to attend. Up north, it was a four-hour drive, but the payoff was a cool five grand and the bragging rights that came with the title.

They had a solid plan and they were original. Robbing gas stations wasn't worth the payoff and banks were too risky—both lessons Wade Brandt would eventually learn the hard way—so Bazooka came up with a fine idea one Sunday morning.

They'd been up for two days when they stopped to refuel in Franklin County. The gas station shared a parking lot with a Cracker Barrel.

They'd been on the road a long while, and the promise of a big country breakfast blew from the air vents and aroused a potent hunger in both men.

"You feel like eatin'?"

Bazooka said he did.

Inside, they found themselves surrounded by a generation of grandmas and grandpas. All of them appeared to be living well. Eating well. Driving nice cars.

Wade asked, "You see how many Cadillacs in this lot?"

That got them to thinking, and Bazooka came up with something.

They finished their meal and paid the bill and left the waitress a generous tip.

"Don't worry," Bazooka assured him. "We'll get it right back."

An hour later, they returned with a handgun and a gallon bag lined with crank residue. Each wore a gunnysack. Bazooka gathered money while Wade pointed hard with the gun. Everything went right. They made three thousand dollars for five minutes' work and got away clean. Things went so well, they tried it again.

"The good thing about Cracker Barrels," Bazooka'd said, "is they's all along the interstate."

That meant good escape routes and the money was easy. They always robbed Cracker Barrels, and always on Sundays. Until the day their luck ran out.

It was Easter morning, and there was bound to be a hungry crowd. They'd scratched out lines of some crank that had a pink look to it on the case of an Elvis CD before they left the truck. Wade went first and snorted and threw his head back and handed the mirror to Bazooka, who did his rail, fat as a pencil, and said, "Long live the king." Then they charged toward the store with a shotgun and a trash bag.

They had problems at the very first table. An elderly man refused. When he shook his bony knuckles in defiance, Bazooka hit him in the head with a fresh bowl of gravy.

Wade saw a man break free and make a run for the lot. Thought about shooting but got distracted. Bazooka had created a fiasco. Everyone made phone calls.

He told Bazooka to hurry, but he was yelling at the old man.

Face red and burned. There was food on the floor, on the old man's clothes. Bazooka stuck a finger in the mess of white hair and plucked out a lump of sausage.

"Dammit, Kincaid," Wade yelled. "Hurry up."

Bazooka stomped toward Wade and kicked him in the ass.

"Shut the fuck up, you dumb bastard. You used my name."

Bazooka walked out, said he was done. But when he stepped out the door, that man who'd made a run for the parking lot had returned with a handgun.

"Get down!" he ordered. But his voice was weak and Bazooka didn't buy it.

"Get down on the ground right now," he said. "I'll shootchya, I swear."

Bazooka threw the man the trash bag and distracted him long enough to grab the hand with the gun and lock it in a vise, throw him off balance.

With his right, Bazooka drove a bone-crushing hook to the side of his jaw and the man went down. Hit the concrete and his teeth spread across the sidewalk like a handful of Tic Tacs. He went out cold, swallowing blood, the gun still in his hand.

Bazooka picked up a tooth and put it in his pocket and walked toward the truck.

Wade chased after Bazooka and cursed him for abandoning the heist, but before they reached the truck, a man who'd seen too many cop shows removed the gun from the first man's hand and began to pursue them.

Wade saw him first and raised the Remington and fired. But his shot was off, and it broke the window of the store. Everybody screamed, and the Good Samaritan opened fire. Windshields broke and vehicles took rounds.

The cops showed up in less than a minute. Both tweakers were arrested.

Wade's record was longer so his sentence was harder. Bazooka got lucky. The man he assaulted refused to press charges. Said all he wanted was his tooth back. Told the cops a good smile was more important.

"Give the man his tooth, Kincaid," the state police said.

Bazooka shrugged. Told the cops he was sorry but he'd swallowed that tooth when he seen them boys coming.

"You what?"

"I ate it. Last thing I wanted was for y'all to find that tooth." Bazooka shrugged again. Said he was sorry.

The next day, the state police took him to the hospital and dressed him in a gown that didn't fit. They wheeled him to a table so a man with cold hands could take an X-ray. When he held it to the light, he frowned. Then nodded and shrugged. The tooth was there, as Bazooka had assured them, a small chip of ivory wedged inside a breakfast turd.

"So here's the deal," Jerry Dean said. He nudged Bazooka with his foot and brought him back to reality. Away from thoughts of prison and his days with Wade Brandt. "He's the one's got the tanks."

"Huh?" Bazooka was lost. "Who's got what, now?"

"The Reverend," Jerry Dean said. "He's the sumbitch that's got all the equipment. Hell, he's got damn near everthing a man would need to live up there."

Jerry Dean saw the girl. But she was not chained up in the Reverend's basement; she was back at *his* place. His mobile home at Helmig Ferry. Though in his mind it was cleaned up. There was a nice deck and a patio. He had a front door that worked.

"What is it you're sayin' exactly?" Bazooka said.

Jerry Dean thought about it. He scratched his neck and shrugged. "Guess I'm sayin' we need ta get rid of that crazy old goat fucker. I dunno, take over his place maybe. Do our own cookin'."

"Say *what*? You'd hafta take out the whole family. My God, how many of 'em live up there?"

"Just him 'n' his old lady. And a big dumb baby of a kid. He's creepy, but he could do shit for us. Be like our butler."

Jerry Dean didn't mention the Reverend's new wife. He planned on keeping her for himself.

Bazooka shook his head. He stood and walked from the table. Farted and drew his pecker from his overalls and peed on the side of his trailer. "Am I hearin' you right?"

Jerry Dean assured him he was. "We got all we need right there. And believe me, I *do* know how ta cook. Trust me, I been helpin' that old bastard long enough I can do that shit in my sleep." He looked at Bazooka. "No more livin' hard. No more killin' turkeys 'n' splittin' wood."

Bazooka said it was a bold idea, but he wanted no part of it.

"Why not? We can grab this tiger by the tail 'n' run with it. Ain't nobody ever gonna know. Nobody. We'd be kings up there, Red."

"What about the cops?' he asked.

"It don't matter none, Red. Cops ain't an issue. Even they won't climb the hill."

"Well," Bazooka said, "you might have one pork under your thumb, but what about them other two? Which one of 'em took it?"

"Red, I do not rightly know. First I thought it was the kid. Now I think it might be the fat one."

Neither man spoke, but it was plain to see Bazooka had rejected the idea.

"It's a good idea, Red. 'Sides, I'm hearin' Wade's gettin' out anytime. Hell, he might be out now."

"Uh-huh. Sounds about right. But your cop buddy ain't gonna like that none. Cuz who's gonna sell that shit with Wade gone?"

"Red, hell if I know. But my cop buddy, he's gettin' real nervous at the thought o' Wade bein' turned loose."

"Why's that?"

"Fuck if I know, Red. Fuck if I know. It's almost like—"

"Brandt's got somethin' on him, don't he? You know that's it."

"Yeah, maybe," Jerry Dean said.

"Maybe my asshole," said Bazooka. "When he gets out, he's gonna be a threat ta anybody who knows about his dealin'."

There were a few minutes of silence between them, awkward silence. Jerry Dean cursed himself for mentioning his plans.

"So now what?" Bazooka said. "Tell me what the next move is. You wantin' ta kill a cop?"

"Not if we ain't gotta."

Bazooka hated cops but he knew when to be smart. He relit

the roach and puffed it a few times but never offered it to share. "We need to scare these cops," he said. "Try that first. Tell 'em they don't cough it up, we kill their families. We do it right, that'll be the end of it."

Jerry Dean said that was good. "Whatchya got in mind?"

"I got a few ideas," Bazooka said. Then he smoked the roach down to nothing and tossed what was left in his mouth and washed it down with a gulp of water from his gas can.

Life on the farm was not the same without Sandy. Olen sat on his sun porch, his face covered with scraggy gray whiskers grown in thin patches, and looked out the window. He watched the fields and the woods beyond. The tree line was many dots of orange and yellow and violet hues mixed with the dying green of Indian summer.

There was a Bible and a shotgun beside him. He would shoot himself on the sun porch. He'd thought about this for a very long time. Many years. Wait until evening. Make a strong drink and watch his last sunset. It was a secret plan he made long ago, secret in the way a man tries to hide his true thoughts from himself.

But in the end, he wasn't strong enough to make it end that way. Or he found something small worth living for. At first, it was the fear of God that kept him from it. Then it was Sandy. Who'd look after her if he pulled the trigger? There was a great-nephew down the line—but he'd learned long ago Jackson Brandt could not be trusted. Now it did not matter. Nothing mattered but that last sunset. And the family who waited on the other side.

He watched the chickens peck bugs out in the yard. Olen hadn't seen Beauregard in a long while, but today he would hunt him down. He was to be the first one shot. It had to start with him. He'd kill the others with the shotgun. He left a note on the front door that said: *Dale, don't come around back. I love you like a son.*

He watched for his stud rooster and looked at the sky as his bladder gave and spread warmth across his lap and he began to cry.

Banks woke up in bed as the news of the suicide at the bank came across his scanner and the first thing he did was call Herb Feeler. Told him he knew it was his day off, but he was on his way.

"Nah, don't do that," Herb said. "Plenty of us headin' out there. Rather you stay home."

Banks was surprised. "I'm right down the road."

The sheriff said he had to go. It was hectic. "Have a good day off," he said, and hung up.

Banks shrugged and saw that it was almost nine thirty. It felt good to sleep in. This was his first real day off in two weeks. He sat up and spun his legs around and grabbed his chew off the nightstand.

The house smelled like syrup when he stepped down into the kitchen. Jude met him with a fresh cup of coffee, and Grace met him with a kiss.

He told his girls good morning and walked outside to pee.

When he came back in, Grace was standing on a kitchen chair, chewing on the head of her doll.

"No, pumpkin," Banks said. "Get down from that chair, young lady."

Grace smiled and shook her head. Banks grabbed her and threw her over his shoulder. She screamed wildly as Banks swung her around and carried her to the living room and dropped her on the couch.

Then he took the doll from her mouth. "Honey, don't be chewin' on this dang thing. It's dirty."

Grace yelled, "Bay-bee!"

"Yeah, honey, but baby's head's dirty. Yucky. You're a big girl now. Big girls don't put things in their mouths."

Grace blew him a kiss and seemed to agree.

Banks returned the doll.

Jude said, "Breakfast."

After breakfast, Jude said she was going yard-saling. Maybe pick up some groceries. She looked at Grace. Then she looked at her husband. Smiled. "You have any plans?"

Banks looked at his wife. He looked down at Grace. "Oh, I see. Mama wants a little *me* time." He winked at Grace.

"Damn right I do," Jude said.

Banks laughed. Told her she deserved it. Enjoy her afternoon. He looked back down at Grace. "Wanna stay with Daddy today, sweets?"

Her little arms shot up in the air. "Dah-dee!"

Mom and Dad laughed. Grace laughed. Banks told Jude to take her time. The two of them had plenty of work to do.

"Ain't that right, little darlin'?"

Grace walked off with her doll.

After Jude left, Banks popped open a beer while Grace stood in the flowerbed and watered everything but the flowers. She watered the sidewalk and the house. She watered Buster as he napped in the shade.

Buster jumped up and woofed. Grace giggled.

"You're doin' just fine," Banks said. He asked her if she wanted to cut grass.

Grace dropped the hose and squealed. She ran to the shed at the end of the yard where a single strand of electric wire separated grass from weeds.

Banks walked over to the well pump and turned off the water. When he got to the shed, Grace was on the riding mower, standing on the seat.

"Now, babe, get down off there, darlin', I'm tellin' you. You can't be standin' on everything. You're gonna fall."

Grace was excited. She screamed and clapped. Banks shook his head and set his beer on the hood. He swept her off the seat in his arms and sat down. He put her on his leg and grabbed his beer from the hood and started the engine and left the shed.

The second time around the yard, he let her drive. As they passed the fire pit, a man stepped out from behind the shed with a rifle and pointed it at Grace.

Banks squeezed his daughter tight and stomped the brake. His beer tumbled from the cup holder onto the grass.

"God no," Banks said, and tried to turn around. Shove his daughter behind him.

The man with the rifle was a huge bulk of a man. Short and thick and powerful. He wore an old potato sack over his head with two eyes cut out and a mouth hole.

"You know why I'm here?"

Banks froze. His baby girl had a rifle pointed at her.

"Do you know?"

Banks didn't say anything but he nodded.

"Y'all best return that money where ya found it. You don't, I'll come back and kill that retard. I'll kill everybody. I don't care if you's a cop."

He took a step forward. Told Banks this was a warning. There would not be another.

Banks saw white skin and freckles and red arm hair.

"You got till midnight on Saturday."

"Where?"

The man backed up and Grace cried for Mama. Banks fought back unadulterated wrath.

"Go back to Helmig Ferry. Like I said, you got till midnight on Saturday."

"I'll be there."

"Yeah, I know you will. Else I kill the retard."

Banks clenched his teeth and nodded.

He spent the evening in the backyard with his family. Jake finished cutting the grass while Banks stood guard at the picnic table. Baby Grace was fine. Banks had convinced her it was just a game. He'd laughed, pinched her cheeks.

She smiled and said, “Dah-dee,” and everything in her small world was perfect.

Her world was the only one that mattered. To protect her world he would kill that man with the rifle. Then turn himself in if he had to. But he would not give back the money. Not to unredeemable filth that cooked meth in his county.

He told his family he loved them and gave his wife a kiss.

“You leavin’, hun?”

“Goin’ out to see poor Olen. Prob’ly sit with him awhile.”

“Oh, that’s so sad,” Jude said. Her voice shared a genuine sympathy Banks could feel. “I know this must be hard on him.”

“It is.”

Jude stopped wiping off the counter and looked up at her husband. “Dale, how does stuff like that happen around here? Old man gettin’ robbed on the side of the road like that? What happened to this town?”

“I don’t know, Jude. Sometimes I don’t even recognize the world no more. I see these kids walkin’ ’round with their pants hangin’ down, their drawers hangin’ out—and the drugs y’know these kids is all on.”

He looked around the room, then bent down to his wife.

“Got called up to the high school, wasn’t two days ago. Kid had naked pictures of his girlfriend on his cell phone. They broke up, so he’s sellin’ ’em. Five bucks a pop ’n’ he’s sendin’ ’em to his friends. Goddamn. What in the hell’s wrong with these kids? I’ll tell ya, it’s the parents, Jude. It is. They just don’t parent like they used to.”

She nodded her head and hoped Jake wasn't one of the kid's friends.

"You got moms working two jobs because the dad's in jail, or he's a drunk. Or a cranker. I hate that shit with a passion, Jude. All these lowlifes drivin' 'round with meth labs in the trunks of their cars. Makes me sick."

Jude picked up her rag and returned to wiping. "I know," she said. "Remember when we was growin' up? All you really had to worry 'bout was drinkin' too much 'n' getttin' pulled over on the way home."

"That's right. That's why God made gravel roads."

Jude laughed. "We had a good time or two on some of them roads."

Banks nodded his head and snorted. Pulled his chew from his pocket and thunked the lid. "Yes, we did," he said. "Many a good time."

He walked toward the door and said good-bye. "I best get."

"Well, OK. We might go 'n' pick up some pizza if that's all right."

"Sure." He reminded her he liked anchovies.

"That's disgusting, Dale."

He grinned and walked out the door, not knowing what the night would bring.

Inside his head, Banks felt like everything was *his* fault. He had to make this right in the eyes of God. He did not think of killing as revenge, but protecting his family. Killing that redheaded bastard was an easy choice.

• • •

Banks left home in his old Bronco with two handguns and a scattergun. Drove into the sun. Reached into the console and pulled out a beer and thought briefly of Bill Hastings as he popped the top. Listened to the sound that made. Unmistakable from other sounds.

Banks raised the can to his lips as the first drink spilled free in a powerful burst. He turned off the blacktop on Highway F and followed that to the state shed where the road split and half turned to gravel. He followed that road and nursed his beer.

He would spend the evening with Olen. Then he would find Jerry Dean and find his way to the rifleman. Banks was prepared and without reservation. A man protects his family, and that's what Banks had the strongest of intentions of doing.

He arrived at the Brandt farm at sundown and stepped from the Bronco with a box of Natural Light. He wore a Kevlar vest under his flannel. There was a Glock on his hip and a snub-nosed .38 on his ankle. Scattergun wedged under the seat.

There was a strong smell of jasmine, and the air tasted like a wave of soft candy.

Banks heard a gunshot and jumped like he'd been stuck with a cattle prod. He dropped the box of cold ones and pulled his Glock from its holster and ran toward the sound. Kept his breathing under control and counted his steps. Ran to the back of the house.

He never saw the note on the door.

• • •

Hastings and his wife had a small house in town, just outside the city limits of Owensville. The closest neighbor was a landscaping business, and they looked to be closed. Jerry Dean drove by the Hastings residence and parked on the shoulder and walked back to the house and hid in the woods.

The sky darkened as he made his way through the backyard. Saw the missus inside. Short shorts, small tits, but damn if they weren't nice—though Jerry Dean was not a picky man, not in the slightest sense of the word, when it came to his taste in women.

Short, tall, big, small, Jerry Dean likes 'em all.

Headlight beams approached as his mind entertained fantasies about Hastings's wife, implausible scenarios only a man in Jerry Dean's position would consider.

When the car passed Hazemann Landscape & Supply—a business run by a mother and son whose bond was the subject of constant gossip—Jerry Dean moved, as fast as he was able, with as much stealth as a fat man at night with a semi-erection could.

Hastings pulled up in his cruiser and put the car in park. Let it run while he looked through paperwork. Talked on his phone. *Hurry up, you fucker.* Jerry Dean had to piss.

Finally, the headlights went off and the engine shut down and Hastings climbed out.

Jerry Dean was pumped. When Hastings walked by, he stepped from the shadows and got him in the shoulder with a stun gun. When he did, the kid's mouth was illuminated with current. Hastings's legs bent into rubber sticks and a grunt of sound was made as he hit the grass.

"Holy shit, I saw lightin' in your mouth," Jerry Dean said. He dragged the kid around the house and removed his handcuffs and secured him to a concrete flowerpot and waited for him to stir.

When the kid could speak, he asked what had happened. What had Jerry Dean done?

"Yeah, sorry 'bout lightin' you up like that, boss. You must have braces or somethin'. I ain't never seen nothin' like that, not in all the times I used this thing."

Jerry Dean explained why he was there. One of those two dipshits stole the money out of Little Buddy's shit box. "*What do you know about that, cowboy?*"

Hastings looked toward the house. From the view on his back, he could not see his wife.

"Oh, don't worry 'bout her, dude. Your old lady's just fine. Yes, sir, just as fine as she can be. But I gotta ask: Does she shave her cooter? Cuz I do believe she looks like she'd be a shaver."

Hastings kicked his leg free and planted a hard shoe in Jerry Dean's groin.

Jerry Dean fell over. "Oh, goddamn, cowboy."

He coughed and rolled on his back and got to his knees and zapped Hastings again. He shocked Hastings's wrist by the metal handcuff, and his mouth sparked and flashed. Like his teeth might catch fire and burn holes through his gums.

Hastings was a strong kid, and after a while he'd built up a real tolerance to electric.

That impressed Jerry Dean, but he assured Hastings his wife would not be as strong.

Hastings threatened Jerry Dean, and Jerry Dean zapped him again. Then his batteries died, and he informed Hastings, in no uncertain terms, what a truly lucky day this had been for him.

"Never buy your batteries from the dollar store."

"I know who you are," Hastings said.

" 'Course you do, tough guy. You's out at my place just the other day."

"It's a shit hole."

Jerry Dean shrugged. "It could use work."

"What kind of piece of shit cooks dope in his kid's bedroom?"

Jerry Dean said he wouldn't know; place was like that when he moved in. And he didn't have any kids anyway. Least not that he knew of. "And not that it's any o' your business . . . but I always been a big believer in the rhythm method myself."

Hastings tried to calm down. Breathed slowly though his nose, like he was concentrating.

"Now, don't go gettin' any big ideas just cuz my stunner died. I still got the Eagle." Jerry Dean patted his hip.

"If you were gonna kill me, you'd've already done it."

Jerry Dean squatted. "And this is a fact, my friend. Had I wanted ta kill you then you would be dead."

They both looked at each other.

"But that ain't what I want."

"What the hell *do* you want?"

"Just to get your attention, partner. You got to arrest somebody tonight."

"What?"

"Listen now, this is a career-makin' case that I'm just givin' you. All you gotta do's show up. You'll see the problem when you get there. Trust me on this one, cowboy; this here bust'll make you a hero."

"What's this about? Maybe you best talk to the sheriff."

"Just show up, that's all you gotta do. Just get it done, sport, and this all goes away."

"All what goes away? Mister, I dunno what you're talkin' about. I don't have no money, and I don't understand none of this."

He looked in the kid's eyes. "No, I 'spect you don't."

Jerry Dean walked back to his truck satisfied that a meaningful conversation had been had. Then he left Owensville. It was dark. The sun was gone, and the stars were sparse. He'd made his intentions to the deputy clear. One of them had the money, and if the money did not find its way back by the weekend, somebody's wife was getting fucked. Then somebody was getting shot.

All this goes away if you arrest Bazooka Kincaid.

He'd told the kid where to find Bazooka. Told him what to do. His words struck a chord in Hastings. "Kid, your old man was a fuck-up. You know it; I know it. Shit, the whole town knows it. Here's a chance to make things right."

Jerry Dean had set a plan in motion; there was no turning back. His destiny waited at the top of Goat Hill. He cranked down the window and felt the wind and made for the deep back pockets of Gasconade County.

• • •

Banks found Olen on the sun porch, covered in piss with a 10-gauge in his hands.

There was a coon lying dead in the yard. Close to the porch.

Olen had fired through the screen door. Blown the top off its hinge. The wooden framework hung down with the torn section of screen still attached.

"Good God-almighty," Banks said, and relaxed his squeeze on his Glock.

"Damn coons. Been tryin' to kill that one for the longest time."

Banks looked at the bloody chunk of meat and the ruined screen door. "You use a big enough gun?"

Olen laughed. But it was a strange, hollow laugh that concerned Banks. Olen wasn't well. The porch smelled like urine. There was an antique cap and ball gun beside him.

"This here was my daddy's gun," he said, and removed it off his lap with considerable effort.

"Let me take that, Olen." Banks grabbed it from his hand. "Damn that sumbitch *is* heavy."

"Yep," said the old man. "They don't make 'em like that n'more."

"No, I don't reckon they do."

It was a double-barrel 10-gauge with dual triggers. One barrel spent and smoking. Banks leaned it against the corner and swore it ran the length of a man.

He pointed toward the old revolver. "What about that one?"

Olen picked it up and handed it to Banks. Told him hang on to it for him. "This was my daddy's, too. Old black powder gun." He laughed. "Smokes like a bastard when you fire it. I was gonna give it to my boy when he was old enough."

He took a deep breath, very quickly, and Banks heard a high sound in the old man's throat. "Guess I waited too long."

The night was black, and the stars were electric dots. Banks watched him watch the yard. He'd never seen Olen without a cap. His hair was long and thin and white. There was a tuft of whiskers on each cheek and chin stubble like untreated wood.

"You gonna be all right, old-timer?"

Olen shook his head, his eyes focused on something Banks couldn't see. "Y'mean, am I goin' crazy? 'M I gonna shoot myself out here in the woods?"

Banks swallowed hard. Said that's what he was asking.

Olen waited. He took his time before he answered. Not because he wanted Banks to hurt. Because he didn't know. "No, Dale, I don't reckon I will."

Both men thought in silence framed by a wall of emotion. An old man at the end of his life, looking back on things he could not change—and a young man looking forward to his future and the things he could.

"I think about you boys, when you's small. The three of you kids was into everthing."

Banks listened to the old man talk. He lived in the past; his sun porch was a time machine, and the memories of his family were all he had.

Olen thought about his words for a long time, thoughts not spoken in fifty years.

"I 'member that day like it was yesterday, when we lost little Gil. I'd been out on that old Ford, plowin', diskin', whatever it had been—and I come up through the low bottoms, through the swag, and sun's in my eyes." He pointed toward the barn. "It was evenin', damn near, and them boys was playin' by that barn with Gilly's kite, and they got it hung in some tree limbs. Tried to knock it down with a metal pole, but Gil touched the power line and it shocked him. Killed 'im."

Olen made a nod with his head toward the yard.

"I come up the hill, there yonder, and I seen it. Didn't know what I's seein' at first. My boy was on fire, dancin', and then there was a *boom*, and he was *put out*. On the ground. Hair burned off at the scalp. Power'd blowed the bottom of his foot off."

Banks couldn't speak.

"You ever smell somebody got burned up? The smell of burnt skin. My boy was covered in blisters, and his face had burned through. I could see his jawbone and teeth. Black skin—what hadn't come off in the melt was black. God it stunk, Dale. My little boy layin' dead cuz I let him buy a damn kite and all I can think is how bad he smells. Those are the last memories of my son."

Hastings left town not long after Jerry Dean. Drove his old Mustang. The car he'd owned since high school. Told his wife he was going to meet Banks. It was important and he could not call him.

He arrived at the Banks home to find it abandoned. Dale's cruiser was parked in the garage, but his Bronco was gone. So was Jude's Olds.

Hastings grabbed the spare key from its hiding place and unlocked the garage. He left Banks a note. They had to talk. If anyone knew what to do, it was Banks. He was honest and decent. The best cop he knew. The kind of father he would be before long.

Becky had surprised him with the news. She was having his baby. She hadn't seen the doctor yet, but those tests weren't wrong—not two in a row. Best she could figure, she was due come May. She liked that. Didn't want to be fat in summer.

It was the best day of Bo Hastings's life.

Hastings let off the gas and the Flowmasters rumbled, expelled backpressure. He eased onto the gravel, careful not to rev the pipes. He passed the turkey farm and parked at the bottom of Hog Trough Road. Sat in the car and gathered his thoughts.

What mess had he stumbled into?

He began the walk up Pigg Hollow. It was cold and dark, but he felt tough. He was well armed. Well trained. And now he had two people to fight for. He'd be a father soon. Had a family to protect and a name to restore. The legacy his old man ruined had newfound potential. Hastings knew it. Believed it. Thought about calling Banks but didn't.

He looked back at his car getting smaller and darker. Coyotes wailed in the holler.

Hastings climbed through ruts and followed washed-out sections of road until it was gone and there was dirt and he could see the outline of a trailer in the glow of dusk.

He approached the mobile home with extreme caution. Drew his gun and released the safety. There were lights on inside. He smelled weed. He pushed his fear aside. Concentrated on the stairs and the screen door above it.

There was a fat beast of a man at the counter. Shotgun beside him. Music playing in the background. Hastings blocked it out. Led with his gun and climbed the steps and opened the door. Stepped inside. Told the man to raise his hands.

Bazooka Kincaid jumped.

"Dammit, boy, you scared the shit outta me."

Hastings grinned and lowered his weapon. "Yeah, that was the point, dumbass."

Bazooka looked disorientated. "What 'n the hell you doin' up here? You ain't suppost ta be here."

Hastings shrugged. "You tell me. Cuz I got no idea. Hell, I thought you 'n' Jerry Dean was tight." He looked curiously at the drying pot plants that filled the room.

"We are tight."

"Well, don't sound like it, bein's he's the one sent me up here."

"Huh?"

"Hell, yeah, he set you up."

"What?"

Hastings nodded. "It's true. He told me to come up here 'n' arrest you."

Bazooka Kincaid was nervous. He knew about the kid and the kid knew about him, but they were not supposed to meet in person. And if so, not like this.

Bazooka Kincaid looked at the joint burning on the counter. And the shotgun. "He told you to arrest me?"

"Don't worry, I ain't gonna. How could I explain it?"

Bazooka looked down at the kid's gun.

Hastings grinned. "Well, I ain't gonna shoot ya, either. Just tell me what the hell's goin' on here. And what's this stolen money shit? I thought we was in this together."

There were large marijuana plants that hung upside down from the ceiling and gave a pungent scent of skunk Hastings had not expected.

Bazooka Kincaid panicked. He did not trust Jerry Dean, and he did not trust the kid. He grabbed the gas can from the counter and doused it over his head and chest. Poured the rest on the floor.

"Get away from me, boy," he screamed, and Hastings took a quick step back.

"Now, calm down," Bo said, shocked. "You're crazy."

"Fuckin' right I'm crazy, you faggot! Now, put that gun down, hoss, or I'll light us both up." He grabbed the joint and drew off it and reddened the end.

Hastings looked back toward the door. Thought about running but fought the urge.

Herb Feeler stepped from the dark hallway and startled Hastings.

"Damn, boss. Scared the shit outta me. So what the hell's goin' on here? What's this about Banks takin' our money?"

Herb Feeler drew his gun and shot Hastings in the neck.

He fell in front of the door and died by the gas can.

Bazooka jumped, stumbled backward.

"Holy fuck, Herb . . . Hell, I thought you was gonna let 'im shoot me."

"Woulda made things easier if he had."

Sheriff Feeler picked up the kid's gun and shot Bazooka once in the chest.

Bazooka dropped against the stove and slid down to the floor. Herb fired a second round into the wall above him.

Sherriff Feeler stepped over Hastings and left the trailer and walked to his horse and mounted and rode down the hill.

Dale Banks left the Brandt farm in his old Bronco and drove home. It had been a long night with Olen. A night of powerful conversation and emotion. He'd enjoyed the time with his friend and was glad he could be there.

Once the night air had turned cold, they'd gone inside. Olen had taken a bath while Banks made a drink with a bottle of Early Times. It was hard to swallow, and Banks wondered if the bottle had gone bad.

He followed pictures on the wall, from room to room, the way Arlene arranged them. They told the story of a family, until it had broken. And then it was the two of them. Picture after picture.

Him on the tractor. With a chainsaw. Or a deer.

Her in the flowerbed. Or the kitchen.

But then the pictures stopped, and there were no more stories to tell.

Banks went back to the kitchen to pour out his drink. He saw a folder on a ledge where Olen sat and paid his bills. There were clippings from Wade's numerous appearances in the town newspaper.

Banks knew Wade would be released in the next few days and wondered how the old man would take it. He'd been gone a few years, but he'd done his time, though much of it had been done in the hole from what Banks gathered.

He picked up a clipping and read it. It was old. Edges of the paper had turned yellow. Wade had outrun the cops in the middle of a snowstorm, but his car ran out of gas. They found him on the shoulder of the road with a stolen TV and a bag of magic mushrooms.

Banks left after that. Drove home and pulled in the driveway and parked and went inside. There was leftover pizza on the counter. He ate a few slices and drank some tea and brushed his teeth and went to bed.

When his phone began to vibrate on the nightstand, he woke up. Almost daylight. Banks cleared his throat and answered: Becky Hastings. She asked if Bo had left. It was late. Was he sleeping on their couch?

Banks wiped the sleep from his eyes and climbed out of bed and walked toward the window.

"Well, babe, he ain't here." Banks almost said he was. Tried to cover for his partner, like any good man would. But this was Hastings. A good kid. There was no need to lie.

Becky Hastings was in tears. Lying in an empty bed, sending messages. Wearing down the battery on her phone.

"Was he supposed to be here?"

"Yeah, Dale, he said y'all had to talk. Said it was important. So where the hell's he at if he ain't with you?"

Banks walked to the bathroom and threw water on his face.

"What time'd he leave?"

"I don't know," she said. "He gets home 'n' he's all worked up 'bout somethin', Dale. I ain't never seen 'im like this."

"What'd he say?"

"That he had to go 'n' talk with you. That's it. He kissed me on the forehead. Told me he loved me 'n' left."

Banks told her he'd make a few calls and call her right back. He hadn't talked to Bo in a while, but they'd find him. Told her not to worry.

He walked down the stairs into the kitchen in his underwear. Held his Glock with both hands, avoiding places in the floor where it was known to creak under stress.

Steph was asleep. Cell phone on her pillow.

Banks shook his head. Checked her window. Looked out into darkness and saw his own reflection. He checked Jake's room and found him sleeping. TV on. Screen blue. Xbox controller on the floor.

Grace was asleep in her own little bed. Dreaming dreams he'd give anything to know.

Banks checked the windows and the doors. Everything looked safe. He walked back to the kitchen and sat down and grabbed his chew off the counter and packed a dip.

It was eight when he left the house in his cruiser. Wore his coat to fight the wind. It would soon be November, and there was a chill in the air that cut to the bone. The sky was gray with a promise of rain, and the roads were slick with leaves.

He drove through a smoke cloud of sweet cedar that blew from the stack of his closest neighbor. It would be a brutal winter. There was wood to split and stack. The ranks were lean. Where had summer gone?

He returned Becky Hastings's call. She answered on the first ring. "Please tell me you found 'im, Dale?"

Banks exhaled a hard breath and told her he was sorry. He'd called twice. Left a message.

Becky sounded stronger than before. Said, "Dale, you're his best friend. . . . Now, you tell me right now . . . is he messin' around on me?"

Banks chuckled. "Well, God no, girl. That boy thinks the world of you." He laughed again. Just to reassure her.

"Well, if that's the case, then somethin's wrong, Dale. *Somethin's wrong.* I feel it in my heart. This ain't like him."

Banks sat at the end of his road with his foot on the brake and listened to her cry.

He said, "I don't know where he might be. He was pretty shaken up over Mr. Hanson. Guess he told you 'bout that?"

"Yeah, he told me and it upset him bad, but he won't talk about it."

"Uh-huh. Guess that don't surprise me none. Bo ain't exactly a talker."

"Dale, I'm worried. Somethin's wrong here, I know it."

"Becky, I promise you—" He saw a note under the windshield wiper that silenced him. He put the car in park.

She'd stopped crying again.

Banks opened the door and stood up. "Lemme jump off here a minute. Call ya back."

"OK," she said, and told him again this wasn't like Bo.

Banks hung up the phone and pulled the slip of paper from behind the wiper and sat down and closed the door and read what the paper said.

Dale,

I know about the money. It's OK I can fix this. Headin' up past Barstow's to straighten things out now. I'll take care of this. Got good news to tell you, too.

Bo

Banks sat behind the wheel and a sensation of absolute fear overcame him. *Hastings knew about the money?* He drove the back of his head into the seat rest and closed his eyes. There were more thoughts inside his head than he was able to accommodate.

Banks pulled onto the road. He did not know where to go or who to trust. *Nobody was above temptation*. Every cop confronted it, and he hated himself for his own weakness. He wondered who the dirty cop was. *Winky?* The son of a bitch complained a lot, but he was true blue. Then again, so was Hastings. Then again, so was *he*.

Banks tore down the two-lane road with the tires barking.

He didn't have a choice anymore. He picked up his phone and called Sheriff Feeler. Told him what he knew: Hastings was missing, his wife worried. Banks had a bad feeling where the kid might be.

"You need to get some guys up there, Herb. I'm a half hour out."

"Where's this at again?"

"Some trailer out past Ned Barstow's turkey farm."

Sheriff Feeler said he knew the place. He'd round up a posse. Help was on the way.

Banks passed Barstow's and saw Hastings's Mustang by the creek. Fought off a gut full of nausea and stopped. Got out. Saw both doors locked. Dust up ahead from the cruisers. He climbed back in the car and dropped it in gear and threw gravel as he climbed the hill.

At the top, there were two cruisers and a Dodge pickup that belonged to the sheriff. Winkler and another deputy, Trent Tallent, stood in front of a trailer with the windows broken out and a yard littered with debris. Everyone looked sick.

Banks knew it was bad. He pulled up in the yard and put the car in park.

Sheriff Herb walked toward him. Told him, "Don't get out."

Winkler, right behind him. "You don't wanna see this, Dale."

Banks pushed Herb aside. "What the fuck's goin' on up here? Where's Bo?"

Winkler stepped in front of him. "Get back 'n your car, goddammit. We got state comin'. This is bad."

Banks shoved Winkler hard, put his weight behind it. Winkler went down in the leaves. Arms fell limp to his side. He stayed on the ground. Yelled at Banks.

"Don't go in there, Dale. The kid's dead."

Banks slowed his steps when he got to the porch. Looked back, saw the sheriff helping Winkler to his feet. He turned toward the trailer and walked up the steps and opened the door. Hastings lay on the floor, the side of his neck blown out. Skin alabaster white, eyes open. Carpet soaked in blood.

Across from Hastings was the rifleman. Massive through the chest and shoulders, with a wide gut to match. Mess of red hair and freckles.

There was a hole in his chest that Banks could see from the door. It was a small red circle, and at that moment it was hard to believe that a small red circle could kill a man.

He turned and saw their faces. Everyone looked guilty.

Banks walked down the steps and away from the trailer and puked in the weeds.

• • •

Many hours later, Banks was back at the station, deep in thought while the state processed the crime scene. They did their own investigation, and it didn't look good. Rumors had already started: off-duty cop found dead beside Kincaid, known felon.

A gunfight late at night in a trailer full of pot plants.

There were things being said about Hastings and none of them good. *There was something about that guy*, they said. *Had a little too much of his daddy in him.* Even in death, they were against him. No one called him a thief, but no one called him a hero.

Herb said, "Looks like the kid took a shot in the neck from close range but hung on long enough to return two rounds of fire."

Sheriff Feeler took it hard, Banks noticed, but not hard enough. He put his hand on Banks's shoulder, promised they'd get through this.

Banks looked back and nodded. Eyes red from hurt.

They sat in Herb's office, drinking hot black coffee and smoking and chewing.

"What're you gonna do about this, Herb?"

He shrugged. "What's to do? We thought we could trust 'im."

Banks looked the sheriff in the eye. "We could."

"Yeah? Don't look like it."

"Herb, Bo was a good kid."

"Was he?"

Banks felt his face tighten and redden. The kid had taken a bullet that was meant for him. "You know he was."

"I know the apple don't fall far from the tree," Herb said.

"You think the kid was part of this?"

Herb stared him down, unflinching. "I think he was part of somethin'."

Banks shook his head. Looked around the small police station. Saw good people everywhere. Looked at the sheriff and saw something else. It was the same pride and guilt Banks had seen a thousand times. Every time he interrogated someone he knew was guilty—especially when they thought they'd gotten away with it.

When Banks turned to leave, Herb said to watch his back.

"And you best watch yours."

"I ain't got no reason to, Dale."

"We all got a reason to."

Hard brown dirt began to soften with each humid drop until it was moist and the wetness soaked in and the dirt became slick and was mud. Ground that had not seen rain in months broke loose and washed down the bluff.

Jerry Dean drove through sage weed and brush to a crook below Goat Hill. He could not chance crossing the ford. Even if he made it without alerting the Reverend, he would not make it back with rain.

Being stuck on Goat Hill was the last thing he wanted now that he could not count on Bazooka Kincaid. At first, it was the promise of easy living that appealed to him—with an abundance of privacy that a compound like Goat Hill provided. But then he'd seen the girl and a sorrow for her washed over him that his heart had never known.

With her in mind, he grabbed an extension ladder from his truck and let it drop across the ford. He brought his gun, a spare clip, and a flashlight that he dropped in the water.

"Kiss my ass," he said as he palmed the rungs with his hands and crawled with his knees. Water deep and black. The beam from his flashlight a speck of flame submerged in a cloud of oil.

A crack of thunder rapped above the treetops and the echo bellowed in the holler. Lightning flashed above his head. He looked down at the ladder and quickened his pace. The hairs on his back felt supercharged.

When he got toward the end, he could feel the ladder slipping. The stream above ran down the rocks and made a channel that washed the mud away.

He crawled fast in the dark, not knowing when the ladder would fall.

When his hands felt the mudbank, there was thunder and the ground trembled. More mud broke loose as he scurried off the ladder and stood, and the ladder fell into the ford before he could grab it.

He looked down and saw it floating. He cursed and held the tree branch and watched his ladder float away. Too late to turn back. By now, Bazooka Kincaid was dead. Or the kid was dead—he hoped both, though it did not matter to him. He'd done what the sheriff wanted. Roughed up the kid. Scared him. Promised he'd be a legend.

He did what it took to get the kid to the trailer. And now, as long as things had gone according to plan, there was one less person who got a cut of the money and a cop to take the blame for killing him.

Jerry Dean dug his heels into rock. Leaned forward. Pulled himself up with trees. He thought about the animals in the woods. The Reverend kept wild hogs and mountain goats and let them run free on the hill. There were other things, too. It was hard to say what might be up there.

He patted the Desert Eagle for reassurance and stumbled across a wad of roots as the hill planed out. He bent at the knee. Caught his breath. His veins pumped with adrenaline.

Jerry Dean pulled a Milwaukee's Best from his pocket and slammed it and belched and said, "Fuck you, Reverend," then chucked the spent can on the ground.

In his mind, after many hits of crank and many beers and several joints, he saw a vision of himself on the hill. He would walk up the front steps and kick the door open and shoot the old man and his wife. Make his way to the basement.

But then he thought about big baby. Dumber than a bucket of screwdrivers. He could not shoot that big dummy unless he had to. Otherwise it didn't seem right. Just shooting a big dumb kid like that. Bad as he might want to.

Something grunted down below, by the ford, and Jerry Dean started climbing. It was hard to say what roamed these woods. The darker it got, the more he thought about why he hadn't thought more about that. Butch Pogue went to auctions. Exotic animals. Jerry Dean knew this, and had somehow overlooked the real significance of one small thing. The Reverend loved his dogs. That's why he locked them up. Not to keep anyone else safe; to keep the dogs safe.

Jerry Dean swore and navigated his way to the farmhouse. Soaked to the bone. The rage of the storm labored his mind. He stopped every two feet, sure he was followed. Soon to be devoured by something nocturnal.

A roar of thunder boomed over the bluff, and the woods carried the sound. Trees shook. Air sour and thick. The face of Butch Pogue appeared in front of him suddenly, and Jerry Dean stumbled backward. Lightning lit up the sky, and the face was gone. There was a great dead tree in its place. Carvings on the bark like ancient scripture.

The rain came even harder. Switched gears.

Jerry Dean took a step back. Looked for something wide with cover. There were caves on the hill. Built into the bluff. Up in the pine thickets. But Jerry Dean would chance a lightning strike before he crawled into a cave at night without a flashlight.

By his best calculation, he was south of the compound. More off-course than he cared to admit. He had not seen the rain coming and had failed to prepare. Thought he'd have starlight. Hand-light. He cursed his luck and waited for a break in rain.

When it came, he hurried. Through the sticker bushes and the thorn patches. Blindly. Arms and hands cut to shreds. Cuts across his face and neck. He slipped in the mud and fell on his stomach. Lay there, fighting for wind.

Jerry Dean rolled to his side and pulled himself to his feet and stood. Turned toward his right and stumbled and tripped until he found road. He smiled despite his misery at this small ray of light. He crossed the road and climbed a fence and walked under power lines between two telephone poles.

The hard dust had turned wet and slick. The grass was a sponge. Jerry Dean crossed the field, and the downpour returned and pounded him in the open with no cover. He ran and slipped but did not fall. When the lighting hit, he could see, and then it was gone, but he pictured what the flash had shown, and walked that way until the grass was gone, and there were sticks, and he was holding on to trees. Limbs and branches poked his face.

Jerry Dean had no record to keep time. The hours since he'd crossed the ford were lost. He kept his mind busy with her face. Her body. He'd seen her from his hiding spot by the woodpile. Watched Mama bathe her in a cold stream of well water. Remembered the steam that rose from her naked breasts and shoulders.

The dusk and the gloom had enveloped him. He staggered through the woods. Through the darkness. In his mind, he saw Mama. She would eat his flesh and suck dry his open wounds. He paused to catch his breath, then moved on. He was glad for the Desert Eagle, but he cursed the rain and the cold and wondered how they would cross back through the ford.

Banks started drinking on the way home from work—he kept a small bottle of schnapps for emergencies. Had to calm his nerves, and for once, the Skoal wasn't working. There would be hell to pay for the man who killed Bo.

He grabbed a box of Natural Light from the garage and walked to the back of the house and sat on the porch. Opened a beer and waited.

When Jude walked out, she hugged him and he cried. Dropped his can on the concrete. "He shot Bo through the neck," Banks said. Jude squeezed him.

Beer poured from the can and filled a crack in the mortar. It formed a pool not unlike the one Hastings died in.

"It'll be all right," Jude said, but she did not have the strength to believe it.

"He was gonna be a dad," Banks said.

Jude cried.

"It's true. Wink was standin' next to him when he found out. He just told me a while ago."

They hugged and shared deep thoughts. Jude was just thankful it wasn't him up in that trailer. Knowing she knew better than to question his heart. He was the rock that strengthened her; he was still the man she married. A father to her children and a man above temptation. How Bo Hastings could be mixed up with a drug dealer she would never know.

Banks was consumed by guilt.

They listened to the wind for a long while. Until Jude stood and said she had to go. She was sorry, but Steph had band practice. It was time to pick her up.

Banks nodded. Told her he loved her. Said he loved the kids.

She turned and walked to the door and stopped. "Dale, what happened to our town? This used to be a good town."

Banks smashed his can and threw it in the yard. "It still is."

• • •

By the time the rain came, the sky was black and he was drunk. Banks finished off the twelve-pack and drank the last few beers from inside the house. When that wasn't enough, he broke out the Jim Beam.

The first drink was a shot mixed with Coke. The second was stronger. By the third shot, he was out of Coke.

His family inside was safe and warm. Banks looked out in the darkness and wrestled his guilt. His questions. He thought about the note Bo left him. If Hastings had been dirty, he would have known—not that he could have been; it was a ridiculous notion to consider. But then his thoughts came back to *himself*. Did anyone suspect Banks was a thief?

If Hastings was the cop Jackson spoke of, then damn if Banks had not misjudged him. But, if Hastings *was* set up, then as far as Banks could tell, that only left one or two guys who could have done it.

Jerry Dean had a partner, besides Bazooka Kincaid, *a cop*. Something Banks had suspected and Jackson confirmed. It could not have been Winkler. He was a hell of a cop, long as he wasn't chasing motorcycles. Not to mention he'd just seen a man shoot his own face off—which got Banks thinking about Wink, which got him thinking about the day Fish died. How Banks had been off work but called Herb anyway. Said he was coming in.

Banks thought hard about that call. About the way Herb had handled it. He wanted Banks to stay home—and a few hours later, there was a rifle in his sweet daughter's face.

Banks leaned back and wrapped up in the blanket Jude had brought him and listened to the rain batter the tin. When the wind blew from the north, the squall drenched his side. He closed his eyes and thought about the Brandt farm in summer. When the world was easy and his memories were shades of gray. In those thoughts, he wondered how different life would be had the right boy died. Little Gil was the sweet one. It should have been Wade in the ground.

Banks asked God how that could happen and wondered if Olen did, too.

He stood too fast and his head spun. Grabbed the support beam to balance. Thunder popped a tight, sharp crack, like a gunshot. Banks swayed. Thought about the crime scene. Saw an image of Bazooka Kincaid, and it all came back in a flash of memory.

Banks had seen him years ago at the courthouse. Banks had been waiting to testify when the prisoners entered, and he walked in. Bazooka Kincaid: on trial for busting up his mother's face with a finishing hammer.

They shuffled him into the courtroom in an orange jumpsuit stretched tight, his hands and feet in shackles, and a look on his face that said they had the right man. He was massive in size, but he'd been robbed of height; his body was squat but powerfully built, as wide as he was tall, with arms and shoulders that looked like they'd been assembled using spare dump truck parts.

Banks sat down in his chair and drank from the bottle and listened to the storm overhead. The kid was dead, and his widow was heartbroken. Banks was heartbroken, too. So was Jude. So was everyone.

Everything in Banks's life was at stake, if only he could take it back.

But he couldn't.

A violent downpour hammered the tin roof of the farmhouse, and lightning scorched the night. The sky pulsed electric veins to a rhythm that would flash and strobe. Mama disappeared to the back of the house to practice her taxidermy.

It was the Reverend's idea. He bought strange animals from auctions and shot them and ate them. It was her job to mount. He showed her what to do. Told her, *Train first with small things*. When he felt she was ready, he would show her the freezer under the stairs.

She sat at her table in the back of the house. Air rank with embalming fluid. Surrounded by dead things: badgers and muskrats and beavers and armadillos. She'd begun to experiment. There was a five-legged rabbit and a squirrel with two heads.

The Reverend was impressed and encouraged her hobby.

Then she heard Butch in the kitchen. He'd come inside the house and slammed the door and stomped his boots on the floor and yelled for the boy to feed the fire. It was raining, and he was cold and worn down and tired of running on crank.

The Reverend opened the fridge and grabbed a piece of chicken and skinned it with his teeth and cracked the bone and sucked out the marrow with a slurping sound that Mama recognized from her room in back. It always made her smile.

Mama watched the rain slide down the window in rolling beads and hummed a sorrowful tune in her throat. She heard the sound of his weight crash into his chair, and she shook her head and hummed and ran her slick tongue across dirty lips.

Summer Atwood dreamed of devils and demons. Tearing and cutting and raping her. Gouging her with their blunt horns, as the walls burned with blistering flames that licked the tongue-and-groove ceiling and burst windows and melted glass.

She cried and shook.

It was dark in the basement and the storm brought things to life. Critters that lived in the dark would move. A mouse scurried over her foot, but she did not flinch. Long ago, she'd grown accustomed to the feeling of quick feet. She watched a shadow on the far wall. Something long and slow crawled across a rank of wood.

There was a door to the right she could not see. It opened, and a wall of light flooded the room. Junior stepped in and walked to the stove. Opened the door and threw in some pig's feet and tossed in a few small logs.

He turned and walked toward the girl and looked at her. Rubbed himself on the outside of his jeans and looked embarrassed.

She wanted to talk to him. Beg him to turn her loose. Tried to yell, but the ball gag kept her quiet. She begged with her eyes, and Junior bent down. Stroked her head.

A mouse darted by and surprised Junior, who stood and turned and left the basement.

Summer leaned back against the wall and watched flames burn the inside of the stovepipe as it glowed red-hot. She closed her mind and went to the only place that could save her. She was home again. Sixteen. Most popular. Before she was a wife and a slave.

Summer Atwood had been a girl once. Had a life other girls envied. Was the girl other girls wanted to be. Her long brown hair fell below her shoulders in loose tangles, impossible to confine or restrain.

She was a cheerleader, and she wasn't perfect, though she tried, but she liked to drink and have sex with boys, and sometimes she would kiss girls, but only sometimes, and only after many cold beers and several minutes of prodding from the others in her group, all of them spoiled unpleasant children who absorbed lives of promise.

The Reverend sought to reform her. He would teach her in the ways of the Word.

He'd seen her name in the paper. *Happy Sweet 16 to Summer Atwood!* And the Reverend got that feeling in his lower gut like a wound that would not heal.

He cut her picture from the paper and held it to the fridge with a magnet and watched her while he ate. Junior watched her, too.

The Reverend knew she'd be the perfect addition to his family. He would take her from the life she lived now. Offer her a new life, *without sin*—and he would have her, day after day, until her belly grew fat with seed and the Pogue family prospered.

When he brought the girl home, Mama knew better than to put up a fight. Said she'd take care of the girl herself. Treat her like a pet. They would keep her down below, in a room under the coal chute. It was small, but it was plenty. And, as fall became winter, and it came time for frost, they would warm her with a rusty vent that pumped in heat from the woodstove.

But the heat drew up the spiders.

The sky had begun to turn orange in the east when Jerry Dean found the house. He was spent from a night of climbing and falling. He made his way to the coal chute and hid behind a group of cedars and caught his breath.

He was close to the house, and it was menacing in all the ways a haunted house was. Thunder blasted off the bluff, and Jerry Dean made a fast trot to the chute. Took cover at the base of a cottonwood.

There was a window behind the tree. Half open. The Reverend in his chair.

Jerry Dean hoped he was sleeping. He waited until thunder crashed, then walked to the window and squatted and opened the coal chute.

Summer Atwood remembered the first time she kissed a boy. At the movies with her parents. She sat in back. With Skip Lundy.

They held hands and kissed in the dark. On Monday, he told his friends there'd been more. Fingers and hands were involved.

Summer hated him for that. She'd have done anything he wanted if only he'd have asked. But he hadn't. He was scared. The first of many lessons she would learn about boys.

In the dark, except for the now-dim flicker of the woodstove, there was no light of any kind in the room. And then the door of the coal chute opened and the rain blew in.

In a flash of lightning, she saw there was a man. Two boots dangling. Legs wiggling.

She shrieked into the ball gag as Jerry Dean squeezed through the hole and dropped to the floor. He hit hard and fell to the ground. When he stood, he stumbled. Called out, "Hey, girl, where you at? Come on, girl, best make this quick."

Summer jerked her hands and dragged the chain across the concrete, and the man jumped. He walked toward her and tripped over the rank of wood.

Jerry Dean cussed, said, "Listen, girl, I'm here to help. The cops sent me. Keep shakin' that chain so I can find you."

She rattled the chain as Jerry Dean's eyes adjusted to the room. He turned and saw the woodstove. Walked toward it and opened the door. Saw flames bright and hot, growing strong with newfound oxygen.

Jerry Dean watched the flames mature into a dominant fire. He turned and walked to the girl. She was chained to the floor in a narrow passage.

As he approached her, she could see from the light of the stove that the police had not dispatched him. He was the mad man from the day before. She shook her head from side to side and screamed into the ball gag.

Jerry Dean raised his hands and shook them. Raised his finger to his lips to shush her. "Calm down," he said. "OK, so I ain't no cop. I just wanted to set your mind at ease, girl."

The girl went to a place in her head that Jerry Dean could not find.

"Listen, I'm here to rescue you. Yeah, I know you seen me kill that pig—but you seen that son of a bitch. You know he's crazy. I had to kill that thing. Ain't like I wanted to." She looked at him, but she did not see him.

"Oh, don't disappear on me, darlin'." He reached out to touch her, and she jumped back and hit her head on the concrete wall.

"Dammit, girl, now calm down." He pulled out his pocketknife and showed it to her. Told her hush. "I'm gonna cut that gag off you, but you *got* to be quiet now, ya hear? You gotta be quiet." She nodded her head.

He tried to cut the strap, but it was made of leather and it was tight against her head and there was no way to cut the strap without cutting her head. There was a small padlock on back.

"No," Jerry Dean said. "Cain't believe that sick bastard has a lock on this thing."

He shrugged and told her he was sorry. Looked her in the eyes and she cried. He wiped the water away with his dirty thumbs. "Listen here, baby doll, I'm here to save you, OK? Gonna get you outta this creepy-ass basement, OK? We're goin' right back out that coal chute in a hot minute, all right?"

She tried to speak but couldn't. She shook her chains and looked down at them.

"Shit," he said. She motioned for him and spoke with her head.

"What're you tryin' to tell me, darlin'?"

She mumbled and raised her hands and threw her head to the left.

"The key?" he said.

She was excited.

He smiled. Asked where it was.

She threw her head to the left.

"Hang on here a minute. I'll ask you a question, OK? You nod your little head up 'n' down for yes. Side to side for no. Got it?"

She nodded her head up and down.

"You know where the key is?"

She nodded yes.

"Is it close by?"

She nodded yes.

Jerry Dean thought for a minute.

"OK, is it . . . five feet away? Yes or no?"

She nodded no.

"OK, so, it's more than five feet away?"

She was getting frustrated and shaking. She screamed into the gag.

"Hey!" Jerry Dean yelled. "Calm down, now. You ain't exactly makin' this rescue easy. Damn, girl, *y'know what I been through?* Now, I'm gonna start walkin' 'round the room. You just yell into your gag there when I'm close."

But she was already yelling, and Jerry Dean threw his hands up. For a brief moment, he thought about saying fuck it and calling the whole thing off.

He walked to the stove and picked up a log and set it gently inside. Laid another one in and stepped back and watched the flames grow. Then he turned, and in that moment she was beautiful. He watched her wet eyes and she blinked once and a tear rolled down her cheek and she looked up. Jerry Dean looked up, too. Saw a golden key hanging from a rusty nail captured in a glint of firelight.

Jerry Dean reached up and snatched the key from the nail, and she cried and turned and gave him her hands. He hoped this was the right key. He slid the key in the hole and opened the lock and her hands were free.

Jerry Dean reached to help her and she grabbed him and squeezed him. Clung to him. It was a perfect moment. He returned her hold. Felt her tears in his chest hair. He promised it would be OK. Jerry Dean was there. He would take her and love her and give her the best life he could give.

Upstairs, the house shook with heavy footsteps. She jumped and stomped her feet and screamed into the gag.

"OK," he said. "I'm goin' up first. When I get up there, I'll reach down 'n' grab you 'n' pull you up."

She shook her head from side to side.

"Listen, darlin', we gotta get outta here *pronto*! I didn't come all this way just to get caught." He turned a log over and climbed on it and heaved himself up through the hole, careful not to lose the Eagle.

• • •

Butch Pogue woke up in the chair when the rain started blowing in and wetting his arm. He sat up and focused his eyes and yawned and stretched. Went to close the window shut and saw flames coming from the basement.

The Reverend jumped up and screamed for the boy. "Junior! House is on fire, you idiot. Get up, you stupid child."

Mama started down the hall. Half dressed, gown open. One of her mammoth tits hanging out. "What is it?" she said.

"That idiot boy o' yours caught the basement on fire. Get down there, boy."

He collided with Junior in the kitchen and followed him down the steps. Junior opened the basement door and stepped inside, and the Reverend shoved him out of the way.

In the glow of the basement, thick with smoke and flame, the Reverend saw his wife's slender legs dangling from the coal chute and then they were gone.

Rain fell hard in dominant sweeping gusts and saturated a knot of branches sheathed in rough patches of bark. Jerry Dean sat against the foot of a dying elm.

Clouds began to split on distant peaks as cold blustery wind pushed down. Drove the rain into his face. It was cold. They waited for the sun to warm them.

Rolling bolts of fire tore loose from the soaring mountaintops and twisted and chewed at the marrow of the cotton ball cloud until the cloud broke in two and drifted apart. Lightning blistered the dull gray sky as he drew shallow breath and the lean air choked his throat with unyielding constriction.

He tried to catch his breath. She was beside him. Knees pulled to her chest. Hair plastered tight against her neck.

Jerry Dean told her he loved her without words. Held her tight while she traced the scar on his collarbone with a finger. His scars were a road map of bad choices that he wore like a badge of honor and polished with pride and shame.

"If we stay here, they'll kill us," he yelled over the downpour.

She nodded like she knew but was tired of running.

Thunder made a low vibrating rumble and they felt the ground quiver and the sky explode and the tree above them shook its branches and soaked them with a potent burst of spray.

He stood, kept his back against the tree and turned to face her. "We gotta go *now.*"

She shook her head from side to side like she wasn't strong enough.

He grabbed her by the arm, jerked her to her feet. "Well, I cain't leave you."

She tried to sit down, but he would not let her. He wrenched her into the open, and they ran toward a broad point of cedars and did their best not to lose footing to slick mud.

The Reverend held the deer rifle across his lap and wiped spit from his chin as Junior bounced through an ancient pothole with cavernous depth.

The tires on the rusted-out truck bounced against the fender wells and the front end heaved. "You done lost her, boy."

Junior turned his head slowly, almost mechanically. Looked at his pa. "Ain't my fault, at all. Wasn't me let the chute open."

"*Goddammit, boy.* Done told you a hun'ert times close that door or she's gonna get out. Now look what we got."

He spit a brown stream of tobacco juice into a plastic cup that overflowed with cigarette butts. The truck came to a crawl as they met the swollen creek—ripe with thoughts of flash flood.

Junior let the front tires drop into the rushing water of the ford, and it felt like the old truck could go.

"Hey, now." The Reverend snarled. "Don't try 'n' cross this mess. She couldn't've made it if we cain't."

Junior found reverse, but the rear tires dug into the thick muck that washed across the road, muddying the rushing deluge that overflowed the creek.

The antique Goodyears spun freely with inadequate traction and the ass end of the truck sank lower—the front axle submerged—as water pounded and milled Junior's door with a forceful cadence.

"We gettin' stuck, boy."

Junior let the truck roll forward, and the engine died. His daddy yelled and dropped his ashtray.

"Sorry, Pa."

They felt the floorboards push up into their boot heels as the water rushed beneath. The front end of the truck shifted hard, but the brake held.

"Get us outta here, boy."

Junior's nervous hand found the key and the engine cranked slow but returned to life—just long enough to offer one final round of sputters before it drowned.

The thin metal floorboards were eaten with cancerous rust and surrendered with little fight. Water broke through and filled the cab.

The Reverend opened his door to escape and more water poured out than came in. He yelled for Junior, but the water pushed against his door with more force than he could match.

"Daddy," Junior yelled.

The Reverend tested the strength of the flood with his eyes. Cried for Junior to stomp the brake. He held the door open with his foot, told Junior stay in the truck till he was free. His grip was firm. He wasn't going to lose that rifle.

The water pushed hard, but the mud held the truck with suction.

That's when the Reverend saw them behind the bumper. It was Jerry Dean Skaggs who had freed his wife; they'd used a fence post to leverage the truck into the mouth of the raging torrent.

They stood in the mud and watched the truck slide into the flash.

The Reverend grabbed for the dash as the cab rolled to the left and Junior's window broke. The truck pitched forward and turned on its side and was swept away.

Jerry Dean took the girl's hand in his. She was trembling.

"My god, girl, we done it. It'll be all right now," he said. "You'll see."

The sky flared above them and the forest quaked with a powerful blast of thunder and the girl's hand was torn from his.

Jerry Dean leaped out of the way and yelled for the girl. Then he saw her. She lay on the ground and blood pumped from her breast into a mud hole that collected water.

"No."

Jerry Dean heard another shot ring out in the holler and knew it was meant for him. He got to his feet, and then he saw Mama standing halfway up Goat Hill with a high-powered rifle.

Raised at her shoulder.

Jerry Dean dove back to the ground as a shot blasted from the top of the hill and blew into a slick chunk of red mud.

He stayed low and ran. Had to make the tree line. He turned to see the girl, and she was dead in the mud. Everything he'd went through to save her just to watch her die.

Jerry Dean ran into the woods where there was no light and paused in the dark with his hands on his knees. Breathing and thinking. He could not cross the creek. That much he knew.

He was trapped. Wet and cold. It would be a long day. He knew Mama would hunt him. She would turn the dogs loose, and they would hunt him. They both wanted to kill and eat him.

Mama walked up the driveway with the rifle, and her face held no expression. She whistled, and the dogs barked and howled. She whistled again and called for Wine, and a fight broke out inside the pen.

Jerry Dean ran up the hill toward the house. Scared as he was, the house was his only refuge. There were weapons in the house. He knew it, though he had never been inside. Never wanted to. The house was looming. Even now it scared him more than Mama or the dogs.

When he got to a thick of spruce, he dropped to the mud and crawled on his belly. He could hear the big woman whistle. Dogs growled and fought and the pen shook.

Jerry Dean ran hard and a flash of lightning cracked and a deep belch of thunder broke loose over Goat Hill. He stumbled across the driveway and tried unsuccessfully to jump a barbed wire fence. Caught his boot on the top strand and landed on his back in wet leaves.

He scuffled for breath while the downpour beat his face. He listened for dogs and heard only his heartbeat. The pulse in his neck throbbed wildly.

He stood slowly and balanced himself on a fence post. Moved toward the house and slipped in the sludge and went down. He cursed and stood as a pit bull rounded the house and ran toward him.

Jerry Dean was a statue of fear. Hands balled into fists. Mouth open.

Then Mama came around the corner, behind the dog. Her expression was unoccupied, but there was hunger in her eyes.

Jerry Dean grabbed the Desert Eagle from its holster and dropped to one knee and aimed at the dog and fired. The dog fell dead in the leaves. When Jerry Dean looked up, Mama was gone. The rain let up for a spell but had returned with fury and strong wind.

Jerry Dean stood on weak legs and ran past the porch, to the corner where Mama had been standing. Stopped and dropped low and poked his head around the side.

He still had seven rounds, but Butch had twenty dogs. Maybe more. Even with the extra clip, every shot counted. He had to get inside. Out of the rain and away from the dogs.

He turned and lightning made a low arc above the trees and there was Mama. Waiting. The vacancy in her eyes filled with hate. She rammed a bone-handle knife deep in Jerry Dean's stomach. Went to split him up and he shot a bullet into her face.

She died on her feet with both hands on the knife.

Jerry Dean stood in the monsoon with the Eagle pouring smoke from the barrel and a hunting knife in his gut. Mama on the ground. Good and dead. Bits of her head washed down the house with cool rainwater.

He felt the knife with his free hand but did not look down. He turned with the gun and looked for dogs. Heard sounds of fighting and knew they were close. He caught his breath. Pointed with the gun. His other hand supported the knife. It did not hurt as bad as he thought it should, and that gave him cause to worry.

Ahead were three dogs in a tug-of-war with a string of the dead dog's innards.

He took a few steps toward the dogs and waited. Raised his gun and stepped closer. The rain let up and there was cloud break. Jerry Dean shot one of the dogs and it fell. The other dog ran off. One stayed and growled at Jerry Dean and he shot it.

He stumbled around the back of the house. Gripped the railing with his hand. Two dogs stood by the back porch and

Jerry Dean shot them both and walked in the house and closed the door.

Inside the farmhouse, Jerry Dean's ears rang from gunfire. Two rounds left. Wine was still out there. They were all out there.

He knocked over tall stacks of magazines and newspapers, but froze once his eyes adjusted to the room. Dead animals lined the hallway in various states of display. There were cats and rats and snakes. There was a horse head mounted above the fireplace.

He walked slowly to the kitchen and held his hand at the wound and puked blood in the sink. Looked down at the protruding bone handle. Blade inside him. When he coughed, the knife jumped. He tried to pull it out, but she had stuck him good. It was a long, broad blade with a gut hook on the tip, and the tip was caught on something. He tugged on the handle, and a wad of bowels inside his belly stretched.

Jerry Dean tasted blood in his throat. He staggered and knocked a pig's head off the counter to the floor. There were jars filled with hog tongues on the table.

Jerry Dean wobbled through the kitchen to a small porch. When he stepped down, he slipped on wet concrete and fell on his back. Gun slid across the floor. He cried. Tried to move but couldn't—his strength was diminished. He watched the bone handle rise and fall with each breath and wanted it free *but once he pulled the knife loose his everythings would spill out.*

That gut hook was snagged on a pile of intestines like a crochet needle caught in a mess of thread. Jerry Dean closed his eyes and counted brown water stains on the ceiling. Bit down on his lip and pushed his brow tight. Worked the knife in and out with a sawing motion. When he tried to remove it, everything went dark and he disappeared into a void between this world and the next.

Jude got up early and put the kids on the bus and fixed a big country breakfast for her husband. But Banks could not eat. He was sick. He'd come in from the porch in early morning. Soaking wet and stinking drunk.

He showered for a long hot while and scrubbed the bourbon from his pores. Today would be hard. According to Winkler, the state boys found crank in Hastings's Mustang. There was also money, but he did not know how much. If the kid was clean, and Banks knew he was, then someone went through a lot of trouble to set him up.

It was cold when Banks stepped outside and walked to the garage. Badly hungover, he drove to town and met Winkler for coffee. But neither one had an appetite.

"What do you make a this, Dale?"

There was a strange energy between them after so much bad had happened.

"I don't know what to make of it, Wink. What do you make of it?"

Winky looked him dead-on. "Somethin' ain't right here, not by a long shot. That's what I make of it."

"You think?"

"There's a nigger in the woodpile is what I think."

Banks took a drink of coffee. "That there is."

"Was your boy part of this?"

Banks shrugged. "I'd like to think not, Winky. But truth is, I dunno what to think no more. Don't know who I can trust."

"Well, that makes two of us, Dale. But I loved that kid. And I'll tell you somethin' else, I'm havin' a hard time believin' the same cop wrestled Fish to the ground was hooked up with Bazooka Kincaid—cuz you know, Kincaid, Fisher, all them boys run together."

"That's right," Banks said. "Always knew you was a good cop."

"Yeah, thank you, Dale. If the kid *was* dirty, he had me fooled. But beyond that, just know that I'm watchin' my back, 'n' I do suggest you watch yours."

That was two days in a row he'd heard that, though with Winky it was genuine. With Herb, it was a warning.

"Yeah, you watch your back, too, 105."

Winkler nodded. They both drank coffee. Banks asked about the suicide of Kenny Fisher. "How you holdin' up?"

Winkler shook his head from side to side and let out a deep breath. "It shook me up, Dale. I ain't gonna lie."

"Damn straight. 'Magine it did."

"Guess there's just somethin' 'bout seein' a man take his life like that. Right 'n front of ya. Guess that's the kinda thing stays with a man. Kinda thing you don't forget."

Banks nodded. "Not to mention you almost died."

The two sat quietly. Knowing they could trust each other, but not knowing what to say. Then they parted ways. Winkler went to the police station, and Banks went for a drive.

They both watched their backs.

Jackson Brandt left his trailer in a minivan with a sheet of clear plastic for a window and a handicap sign that would have swung from the rearview mirror had there been one. It was his mama's van, though she could no longer fit behind the wheel to drive it.

Jackson's mama was five hundred pounds and seldom went out. But when she did, she would crawl through the van's sliding door and sit on the floor. Her size was a burden, except in snow, when the weight came in handy and provided traction.

But the times she left her home were few. Once a year, on her birthday, they would go to her favorite restaurant. Beyond that, she did not leave the trailer, and when inside the trailer, there were certain places in certain rooms she could not walk or she would fall through the floor.

Once, she *had* fallen through. She'd opened her closet and a mouse shot by; she jumped. But when she did, the floor shook and gave way and she fell through it. Broke her leg in two places. They cut the rest of the floorboards out with a chainsaw and lowered her to the dirt. Drug her out from under the trailer with a log chain and the neighbor's tractor.

Jackson knew things were about to go bad; there was no direction left. The holes they had dug for themselves were growing wider and deeper, and now Fish was dead. He'd killed his cousin and that old woman from the bank. Then he'd turned the gun on himself, or so the rumor stated.

It was all over town. News like that spread faster than a flash fire in a match factory.

Jackson could not believe it, and those thoughts consumed him. *Why Fish hadn't taken the crank from his shed and run.* There were bound to be places in the hills for a man like Fish to hide. There was no need to make a stand.

Besides, Fish would not have done himself in if he still had crank—that much Jackson knew. That he had removed himself from this earth so dramatically told Jackson Brandt that Fish had not found the cooler.

Those thoughts played in Jackson's mind in broken fragments. He did his best to connect them, because Jackson had his own suspicions as to what had happened.

Fish had murdered his cousin but did not have the strength to shoot his wife. Which, now that he thought about it, could end up being good for *him*, for Jackson. With both Early and Fish out of the way, maybe *he* would have a chance with Raylene. Long as Jerry Dean didn't swoop in like a knight in shining armor and steal her away—though in Jerry Dean's case, he would be a knight in shining tin foil.

Jackson smirked at that, the thought of Jerry Dean playing hero.

Still, he thought about that cooler in the shed. He had opened it himself. Seen a gallon bag with a block of crank that held the shape of a small boulder. It was hard, with a rounded edge; it looked like a lump of soap.

But then, maybe the cops had found it. Though Jackson did not know. He was thinking fast and driving fast. Making notes from observations along the way.

He met Banks at a dry creek bed on Brick Church Road.

Jackson said, "I followed the sheriff, man. I done whatchya asked."

"And?"

"Well, he's got this gal he sees at the Fuel Mart. But I'm sure you know about that."

Banks raised his eyebrows, and Jackson said it was true.

"He's been seein' her on the side for a hell of a long time. Least that's what Fish says. He's the one sells her dope."

"You mean *used* to sell her dope?" Banks asked Jackson if he'd heard about Fish.

Jackson swallowed hard. Said he had. Said it was a shame how it had all went down.

"A *shame*? That piece of shit tried to kill a deputy."

Jackson was surprised, genuinely. "Holy shit. I dunno, man. His wife, she run off 'n' left him. Man, pussy makes you do strange things."

"Yeah 'n' so does crank."

"Yeah, I know, and I learnt my lesson the hard way, man—that's why I'm done with that shit. *I swear.*"

Banks ignored him. "So what about Feeler? He's got him a girlfriend. OK, what else? She a crank whore? Are they . . . *both* usin'?"

• • •

Banks cocked his head to the side and felt his jaw slide open with the sudden realization of all he had learned. "Is Herb smoking that shit himself?"

It was an obvious question and Banks was disappointed in himself for failing to consider it.

"Now, how would I know that, man? All I know's what Jerry Dean tells me 'n' what I seen with my own eyes." Jackson looked down, uncomfortable.

"Go on," Banks said.

"OK, but," he paused. "I hate ta say this, I do. But the sheriff, he went up that hill, man. Past Barstow's . . . but I stopped right there. Cuz I knew where he's goin'. Up ta that old trailer, only place that road goes."

Banks sat in silence. Looked out the window. Thought about the things he'd heard. He thought about the things he'd seen and the things he already knew. Remembered Herb Feeler and his rise to power—years back—and how it all began with Jerry Dean's arrest.

"Who shot the kid?"

Jackson shrugged. Said he didn't know, and Banks was pretty sure he didn't. How could he? The only one who knew was the one of three people from that trailer still alive.

Three people can keep a secret if two of them are dead.

Banks realized how things must have happened. Maybe Herb had caught Jerry Dean with more than a bald eagle, and that led Banks to deeper thoughts and more realizations, until suddenly, he saw how everything was connected.

Jerry Dean was a partner to Bazooka Kincaid, who was

partners with Wade Brandt. There was an unbroken circle of business cohorts and Banks could see them clearly.

Jerry Dean and Bazooka did the gathering and cooking, so they must have had a man inside. Like a prison guard. Someone to mule in product for Wade Brandt to distribute.

The meth business in Algoa was thriving, and Banks was sure he'd just found the source.

"Bazooka Kincaid lives up there," Jackson went on. "He's Jerry Dean's partner, y'know. 'N' he's crazier than a shit-house rat. Hell, he put his own mom in the hospital."

Banks agreed with a nod and thought about what he would do. He had a few questions. "So how's the shit get inside Algoa?"

Jackson shrugged but Banks saw through it. Told him spill his guts.

"Listen, I keep talkin' 'n' they find out, I'm a dead man."

"Ain't nobody gonna find out. This is b'tween you 'n' me. OK?"

"Yeah, sure it is."

"You can trust me."

"Ha. Yeah, sure I can. Listen, mister, in this business you cain't trust nobody."

Trust me. Banks thought about how absurd that must sound coming from the man who'd gotten all of this started in the first place. How his greed had gotten the best of him, despite his personal beliefs and his best intentions.

"No, I reckon you can't trust nobody who smokes that shit. But I don't smoke that shit. And right now, you gotta trust me cuz I'm all you've got."

Jackson nodded.

"How they get this shit inside the prison? They got a guard?"

Jackson nodded.

"And who might that be?"

"Listen, man, I ain't no rat."

"No, Jackson, you ain't—and for that I do respect you. Tell ya what: you stay off that pipe, and I may even letchya mow my lawn."

Jackson showed Banks a dirty grin and thought for a minute. "It's this guard, man, Ray Hall. He's the brother to Jerry Dean's cousin's wife."

"Jerry Dean's . . . cousin's . . . wife?"

"Yes, sir, that'd be Darlene. She's been writin' Wade Brandt letters. Least that's what I hear."

"She's writin' Wade Brandt letters?"

"That's what Jerry Dean says. And if you're curious as to how that came ta be, I can tell ya right now. Save you the trouble of wonderin'."

"Save me the trouble, then."

"It was her brother, the guard."

"Was, huh."

"Yeah, Ray. He set the whole thing up, introduced 'em. And he's a strange one, too; Jerry Dean'll tell ya. Says he went ta Ray's place one morning 'n' when he stepped on the front porch he saw Big Ray walk through the kitchen in a dress. So Jerry Dean knocks on the door. Few minutes later, Ray opens it. Says he's been sleepin', but Jerry Dean said he forgot to wipe the rouge off his cheeks."

Banks scratched his chin and shook his head and reached for his can of chew.

"What the hell's wrong with you boys?"

Jackson didn't know. "Jerry Dean says Ray must've gotten too comfortable puttin' things in his anus. Somehow that must've opened up a whole new side to 'im."

Banks shook his head, thrown off balance by the news. "Where can I find this sick bastard?"

"Hell if I know," Jackson said. "But Ronnie and Darlene live out at Helmig Ferry. Sometimes he goes out there."

Banks nodded. "Uh-huh, Helmig Ferry. And why don't that surprise me?"

"Listen, man, all I know's Wade's gettin' outta prison this week. Hell, it might be tomorrow. Hell, man, he may already be out. But all I know's that's got everybody worked up."

"Who's everybody?"

"Hell, man, I dunno. It's got your boss worked up, 'n' that's got Jerry Dean worked up."

"What's Wade gettin' outta prison have to do with anything?"

Jackson shrugged. "Mister, I don't know. It's the sheriff. I think he's got big plans. Wants to run for governor or somethin'. Jerry Dean says he wants ta be done with this business once 'n' for all 'n' he's tyin' up loose ends."

"Jerry Dean told you this?"

"He told me some, cuz he talks when he's wired, but some conclusions I drawed on my own."

"It's them conclusions you drew on your own that I'm worried about."

Jackson almost looked offended, but kept going. "Listen, man, I think maybe Wade's had enough. He just wants outta the life, same as me. Least that's what I gather."

"What's Jerry Dean think of him wantin' to go straight?"

"I don't think he gives a shit, man. He just does what the sheriff tells him—but the sheriff, he don't like it none. You ask me, I think they might kill 'im."

Banks closed his eyes. "Sweet Jesus. All of this killin' over crank."

"They say they cain't trust 'im."

" 'Course not. He knows too much. Now he's a liability."

Jackson shrugged and looked out the window. "Sounds like we's all liabilities."

Banks had managed to extract more information from Jackson than he'd expected. "You done good, convict."

Jackson ran his tongue along the inside of his mouth and caressed his top gum.

"Am I free to go now, man? Cuz, listen, I know what happened to your guy up there 'n' I'm real sorry 'bout that. I just want outta this mess. I'm done with crank. Done with everything, except alcohol, cuz that ain't outlawed yet. But that's it. I'm just gonna drink from now on—and I won't drive, neither. I just wanna sit at home and drink and work on lawnmowers, man. I know my way around them small engines and shit."

Banks told him to go. Keep his nose clean. "I don't have to tell you not to talk about this."

"No, sir, you do not. Far as Jackson Brandt's concerned, none of this ever happened."

"And you best be done with crank. Not many tweakers get a second chance."

"Oh, I am done, mister. That's a promise. I won't never do crank again."

He left his meeting with Banks and drove six miles to a gravel road and parked his mama's van on the shoulder and removed the key. C & K Towing sat to his right. Through a half-mile of dense woods, more or less, though Jackson Brandt had never been a good judge of distance.

He walked through a ditch and stepped over sagging strands of rusted barbed wire and made his way through the woods. The trees were naked and bare limbed and offered modest cover. So he hid behind cedars, of which there were many, strewn throughout the property in small abundant patches. Humming above him was a three-phase power line, loved by the birds that picked berries from cedars and shat them and produced new cedars, so that they had accumulated throughout the area and, over the years, produced a tapestry of green that never had a leaf to shed.

They provided good cover on a fall afternoon. Jackson took his time and walked leisurely, until he found the beginning of an ambitious junk pile. Small things did their best to trip him. Old fenders and hoods and axles. Motors and transmissions. There were cars that were wrecked beside cars that weren't.

Jackson squatted in leaves. He was close to the shop, and he was cautious. Couldn't hear anything or anyone. No voices or music, no sound of air tools. He did his best to watch for people, though his focus was the cooler. His mission: find the contents of the shed. That crank was his pot of gold, waiting at the end of a piss-yellow rainbow.

There was a Toyota pickup with a window AC unit in the bed that Jackson thought he knew. It looked like the one from Fish's shed. He squinted and looked as close as he could, but from that distance it was pointless.

When he saw a Snap-on toolbox with a dent in the lid, he knew that he was close. His heart rate began to soar. Palms slick with sweat. Casually—and with great attention being paid to the fact that whoever worked at C & K was probably on a lunch break that was soon to end—he took a few quiet steps across slick stones lacquered with years of oil stain and crouched beside a stump.

He lay on his belly and crawled, in broad daylight, on an imperative mission to find the cooler. He fought off thoughts of Banks pulling up and focused on the crank.

And then he saw it, on its side. By an air compressor that didn't work.

Jackson crawled faster, and less cautiously, until he was hunched and fast walking. Stooped over. Head glancing from his left side to his right side. And then he was there, standing beside it. Jubilant with emotion but unconvinced it was true. Afraid when he opened the cooler, the crank would be gone.

He squatted to the gravel and stood the cooler up and removed the lid. Hands trembling. And then it was there, in front of him, all the crank he could dream of.

His face lit up with wonder.

Jackson stood and grabbed the cooler and ran before he could stop himself from it. It felt good to have this. The crank was a blessing. He would sell it and buy something nice for his mom.

Buy a place for himself and Raylene. Because the more he thought about that cooler, the more he thought about the life he could give her now that he had it.

He stumbled from the woods, sure that Banks was waiting, that all of this had been an elaborate ruse.

But it wasn't, and Banks was not there waiting for him with handcuffs.

Jackson climbed in his mama's van and set the cooler in the passenger seat and started the engine and put the shifter in gear and pulled on to the road.

Jerry Dean woke up in a slick gleam of sweat. He'd dreamed about his mama. They bounced around when he was young. He'd grown up in some rough places and he never knew his daddy, but his mama said he'd been a vicious man.

She was raped when she was fourteen, and Jerry Dean was the result. She let him know that early on and reminded him often. His mama was a drunk. She'd come home from the bar with cum stains on her shirt and make Jerry Dean rub her feet.

Some nights, in the haze of drunken moments, she'd come onto him. And most nights, he'd resisted. But then she disappeared. Ran off with a truck driver named Papa Bear, and the last time Jerry Dean saw her, he was young.

But in his dream, they'd been a family—at a long table—and his daddy was a handsome man, well tailored. His mama was slim and elegant and beautiful.

It was a Norman Rockwell painting had they not been in a mobile home.

And then Jerry Dean woke up with a hunting knife in his gut. He turned and brought himself slowly to a crouch and looked out the window. The sun was bright. He reached for the Eagle and stood painfully and hoped nothing fell out of his stomach.

He reloaded his gun and opened the back door and walked down the steps. Stood in the mud. It was cold. Wind bitter and sharp. He looked for dogs and saw Mama's legs sticking out from beside the house.

He walked to the shed with the gun held in front of him. He felt alive in the cold, like there was a strong chance he might survive. Olen's Dodge was in the shed, and Jerry Dean prayed there was a key.

Then he saw the truck. Junior had removed the doors and the hood.

Jerry Dean was relieved to find a key, but that simple asshole had removed the seats. He would be forced to drive the truck on a five-gallon bucket, and the only one he found held remnants of the pig he'd slaughtered just the other day.

He returned to the truck and dumped out the pig guts and set the bucket on the bare metal floor. Lifted the shed door. Thought about the pound of crank in the Reverend's lab, but knew he could always come back.

But first, there was that knife in his midsection. And before that, there was the ford he would have to cross on a five-gallon bucket if he wanted to make the hospital.

He already knew what he would say. There'd been a pumpkin-carving accident at his cousin's place. They would have no reason to doubt him. Long as he didn't pull up in a stolen truck without doors or a hood.

Jerry Dean climbed into the truck and lowered himself carefully to the bucket. The top was small and his ass hung over the sides. When he started the truck, the shed filled with diesel smoke and he revved the engine and relaxed. Breathed a sigh of relief and pulled out of the shed and cut deep tracks in the mud.

The storm would be great for his plants. One good soaking before he picked them.

Good Lord, it would be a glorious crop.

When he turned right, he bounced through a deep hole that tested the truck's suspension and the bucket slid out from under him and he fell on the floor. He could not see to drive. He hit the key and killed the engine.

The truck bucked as it came to an abrupt halt, and Jerry Dean stood and reached for the bucket. He set the bucket down and planted himself on it and pulled the seat belt tight across his chest. As he turned the key, a Rottweiler of considerable size ran to the passenger side and jumped in. Lips pulled back, teeth gnarling.

Jerry Dean, seat-belted and trapped, reached for his gun as the dog attacked. He fought him with his left arm and unholstered the Eagle with his right. Shot the Rott in the stomach.

Blood sprayed the inside of the windshield, and the dog fell dead on the floor.

Jerry Dean started the truck and pulled away. More dogs ran toward him.

"Come on, you motherfuckers."

He shot at a dog but missed. Blood ran down his arm in every direction. He aimed and shot again, and the mutt went down. To his right, another dog ran alongside the truck and tried to jump in. Jerry Dean slowed, and when the dog jumped up, he killed it.

He shifted into second and the ground was slick and the truck slid. Jerry Dean could drive no faster. With every bump, the knife moved, and when the knife moved, it cut a little deeper.

Beside him, a brindle pit ran up to his door. He aimed and shot, and the pit fell to the ground and howled and became food for the other dogs. Jerry Dean could not believe all the dogs he'd killed. His ears rang. He hoped he hadn't damaged his hearing.

He got to the bottom of Goat Hill, and the girl lay dead in the mud. He looked down at the knife and cussed her. He should have waited in the basement and shot them all.

Jerry Dean straddled her body with the tires. The rush of water was strong, and it was deeper than it was the last time he'd crossed. The hood would have gone under if there had been one. The inside would fill with water and pass through the cab. He gripped the wheel.

Why'd that dumb son of a bitch take the doors off?

He pulled the belt tight and gritted his teeth. Looked down at the knife and the dead dog. Spat. The pain he felt was immeasurable. He could not believe he was still alive.

Take a lot more than a knife wound to stop Jerry Dean.

With great reluctance, he engaged the four-wheel drive and pulled into the ford. The sound of the water was thunderous. He eased the truck into second gear and pushed the pedal down. Water slammed him from the side and blew the bucket out from under him. He jammed his feet into the floor and pushed his back against the cab. The Rottweiler disappeared through the open door, and he saw the gutbucket bobbing downstream.

The force of the wave was great, and the water from the ford was freezing. Jerry Dean squeezed the wheel with all he had. The might of the water pressed against the bone handle, and he howled in maddening pain. He stomped the pedal and the fenders went under and the engine was submerged in creek water—but the Dodge pulled hard and the tailpipe pushed a gush of black smoke under the waves.

The truck bucked and jumped and the ass end slid off the ramp, but the weight of the Cummins held the front end down. Both wheels burrowed deep into gravel and pulled the truck from the ford.

Jerry Dean saw a rutted field of hacked cornstalks and felt his life seeping from the wound. He could feel nothing below his chest. When the darkness came, he relaxed his grip on the wheel and slumped over, but the seat belt held him up and the truck ran for a hundred feet before it met the cornfield and lurched to a stop and the engine died.

• • •

Kent Pace was a pumpkin farmer in the low bottoms of the county. After the creek broke its banks and the flood came, he found the bed of an old pickup truck in his yard. He grabbed his son, and they rode the four-wheeler to check the fence lines for breaks and to discover what new adventure the storm debris had brought.

Kent followed a road of deep mud to the edge of his field, and they climbed off the machine and walked toward the creek. There was a heap of metal around the bend, wedged between a tree and an overhang of ancient rock that jutted from the bluff.

He held his son's hand and they walked toward the truck and he saw there was a cab. It was the front of the truck that belonged to the back of the truck in his field.

There was a dead boy floating inside.

Kent crouched down and studied him. Stood and raised his hand to shield the sun. Looked up the creek to Valentine Ford. Set his son on the four-wheeler and used his cell phone and called the police. Told them his name. Where he lived. There was a body in his backyard that washed down from the ford.

"It's strange," he said. "Only one place to cross up past me, 'n' that's Goat Hill."

Farmer Pace said they'd better send somebody. He had a bad feeling about that truck.

The Reverend scaled the sandstone wall of rock and crawled through the woods. His eyes were swollen from the tears he'd shed. He'd lost a wife and one son. Was betrayed by another—*Jerry Dean Skaggs.* So many times he'd wanted to tell him: *I'm your father, Jerry Dean. This here path you must take.*

It was a righteous path that led to untold glory.

But Jerry Dean was a sinner and a nonbeliever. The Reverend would need to convert him. Wash him free of lust and want. Baptize him at daybreak in the waters of the ford.

But things had not worked out that way. Any plan he'd had for salvation had failed.

Butch raised his fists to the sky. "Jerry Dean," he yelled, "how could you betray me?"

The Reverend climbed rock hills and stumbled through washed-out ditches. Shivering from the cold. His shirt torn from his body in the flood. The sun was distant and gave little heat.

Below he heard sirens. They had found Jerry Dean, and somewhere poor Junior lay drowned. His new wife's body had fallen by the water's edge, and the Reverend yelled for Mama. His broken voice echoed in the holler.

Mama had betrayed him, too. Shot his wife in one of her fits. She'd been known to have them. She'd killed his first wife, too. Jerry Dean's mom. She'd been the first one he'd taken, years after he had raped her and given her a son. He swore one day he would have her again, so he waited for her to raise the boy. Then he kidnapped her and brought her home and locked her in a cage.

But Mama's insecurities boiled over, and jealousy got the best of her. One day while the Reverend went to town, Mama shot her with a pistol and fed her body to the dogs.

Mama promised him she'd changed, but the Reverend was a fool to believe it.

He struggled for breath and climbed until he found a well-trodden path used by hogs. It was heavily furrowed, and the mud holes filled with rain. He leaned against a tree to rest, and a loud noise crashed behind him. The Reverend held his breath, made his body still. Something behind him grunted loudly.

The Reverend looked from around the tree at a wild hog that hadn't seen nourishment in a great while. It came at him with yellow eyes and a thick rancid froth at its mouth and slammed him from the side.

The Reverend cartwheeled through the air and landed on his stomach, wind forced from his chest. He heaved, tried to stand, but the hog snorted and rammed him with its head. Drove tusks through yielding flesh.

The Reverend sucked air and hollered and ribs broke loose from their cage and punctured lungs.

He rolled to his side and began to stand when the hog threw his head down and butted him. Knocked him back to the mud and crushed bones in his face. Wild sounds came from the beast as it bit him.

Another boar came running, and it charged the hog that had attacked the Reverend. There was a powerful conflict of brawn. Hogs crashed to the mud. Fought with their heads and plunged tusks into hide.

When the Reverend tried to stand, he was free. But he stood in great pain and bled abundantly from the wound. Broken ribs floated inside his lungs. He coughed, and blood burst from his mouth in a luminous mist and stained the leaves.

He made his way up the hill, and when he passed the pen, he saw his dogs were free. He found two dogs in the driveway. Both dead. He shook his fists and cursed Jerry Dean—and then he saw Mama, beside the house. The dogs had eaten the parts of her face that had not been shot off.

The Reverend limped into the shed and returned with a can of gasoline. He saturated the shed and made a wet line to the house. Doused the kitchen and the living room and took a seat in his chair. His family was gone. They waited for him on the other side.

He reached beside him and picked up a glass pipe and poured crank in the bowl. Leaned back in his recliner and kicked over the gas can with his foot.

He struck the butane torch and burst into flames and burned in his chair. The fire gave voice to his powerful screams, and the house burned up around him.

And there was no God waiting on the other side to call him home.

Banks called the station and said he would not be in for a while; he was taking a few days off. They said that was fine. They understood. Deputy Trent Tallent would fill in for Banks. He said he could use the hours.

Banks looked into Sheriff Feeler a little closer and did not like what he saw.

Herb was as crooked as a dog's hind leg. That much Banks knew. Herb had a wife and a son—and according to Jackson, as well as his own detective work, a girlfriend he kept on the side.

Her name was Sue Ann Johnston. She was thirty-six but looked fifty-six, had two busts for possession and a face that showed a road map of drug use. She had a daughter that her mama raised and a tattoo on her wrist.

It was a butterfly that had been poorly constructed. Or perhaps it was a flower; Banks couldn't tell. But she had looked at him queerly when he entered the Fuel Mart in his uniform and bought a can of Skoal.

Banks met her cautious stare with his own and wondered if she knew. About the money. Or the kid. Would she call Herb Feeler as soon as Banks left and tell him where he was? He compared evidence with instincts and allowed his curiosity to drive him. He had a thousand questions but no one to ask.

How deep into the rabbit hole had he stumbled?

Banks dug a little deeper and learned she was kin to Jerry Dean. He smiled to himself as the pieces fell in place. They were a cluster of lowlifes that ran in circles. Some connected by blood, some connected by drugs.

But once Herb's political ambitions had come calling, he'd wanted to put his thug life behind him. Either way, Wade was a millstone once he was free. Now the kid was gone. So was Bazooka. Wade might be next. Which left Jerry Dean, and Banks wondered if Herb didn't have plans for him as well. One way or another.

Banks had a bad feeling about Herb Feeler that kept gettin' worse. He would do what it took to keep his pockets swelled. He had a ranch to pay for—and a wife and a kid and a crank whore—and the salary of an elected official in Gasconade County would only stretch so far.

It was easy to see how things had happened. Banks knew that as well as anyone.

But Herb had killed the kid. Banks knew it and could not forgive him. He also knew he'd best act fast before Herb started thinking about ways to get rid of *him*. Because sooner or later, if he hadn't already, he would.

Jerry Dean Skaggs woke up in a hospital bed with his hand chained to the railing and a colostomy bag attached to his gut. It had been a long two days. The memories of what he'd seen and felt were dim. There'd been an ambulance ride and bright lights and strange voices. Doctors wearing masks.

But the rest was a blur of bewilderment and painkillers.

He took a deep breath and winced at the pain and watched dark fluid drain from under his gown. It filled a clear plastic bag that hung from his bed. He could not believe he was alive. He smiled despite the handcuffs and the bag and hoped he could make a deal.

Herb Feeler was the man they were looking for. Jerry Dean had done no wrong.

Except for stealing the truck and the tanks and killing those dogs. Then he thought about Mama and winced. Then he remembered the Desert Eagle and hoped it was lost in the ford.

A man walked through the door and introduced himself. His name was Dr. Chadwick. He said Jerry Dean was lucky.

"How you figure that, Doc?"

"Well, you're alive, aren'tchya?"

Jerry Dean closed his eyes. Said that might be true, but things could always be better.

He looked down at his colostomy bag.

"You got a few people wanna talk to you, son."

Jerry Dean nodded. "Reckon I do."

"You feel like talkin'?

"Reckon I don't."

The doctor said, "OK." He checked the numbers on a machine and grabbed a clipboard and left the room. Told Jerry Dean he didn't blame him.

Jerry Dean had spent the whole morning thinking until he'd come up with a plan. He would not talk without his attorney. Not that he had one or could afford one. But that was the best he could do until he figured things out. Perhaps he would represent himself. Be his own attorney, and if he lost, he would demand a mistrial on the grounds of inadequate council. Jerry Dean knew a thing or two about the law.

This was not his first rodeo.

The best idea he came up with was just to play dumb, which would not be too hard. He'd say he smoked crank with the Reverend, long into the night, until the Reverend had finally lost it. Then he'd shot his wives and drowned his son. He'd even killed his dogs.

Son of a bitch was crazy. Jerry Dean had been lucky to survive.

That was a good plan. He'd done his best to save the girl. He would paint himself a brave man. Maybe the town would, too. He'd get a pardon from the mayor. Or a key to the city, however that worked. After all, he was bringing down a crooked cop. Maybe he'd be famous. Do interviews. He thought about a piece of land he would buy and the double-wide he would put there. Hell, he could pick up Earl Lee's place cheap, now that he wouldn't be needing it. He could buy it from Bay Bank for a song.

And then he thought of all those beautiful pot plants waiting for him to harvest.

Jerry Dean smiled again at the thoughts of his future. Smiled so hard it hurt. He'd do his best to lead by example from here on out. And perhaps one day, when this was all said and done, and the fame had worn down and the dust had settled, he would find himself a new girl to replace the one he'd lost. Enjoy the hero's status that bringing down police corruption would provide.

He coughed and his gut filled with pain and the bag moved. Jerry Dean closed his eyes as he floated toward a deep siesta and dreamed the dreams of champions.

Wade Brandt left prison a free man and made a promise to himself never to return. He was leaving Algoa for the last time and never coming back.

He had made that promise before—and inside he'd done what it took to survive—but this time, he swore, was different.

He would walk out those gates a changed man. Into the arms of the woman who had saved him, through her letters and her phone calls. She had even sent pictures, though in them she'd been younger and prettier and substantially thinner.

Wade Brandt left Algoa in faded Levi's that threatened to slide off, a pair of steel-toed boots, and a T-shirt advertising Snag's Pool Hall that read LIQUOR IN THE FRONT, POKER IN THE REAR. It was his favorite shirt when he went in, but since he'd lost weight it was a size too big.

He passed the main gate and a thin black guard with skin stretched tight across his face warned him not to come back. Then Wade stepped into that harsh golden sunlight and what he saw stopped him in mid-stride like a brick wall.

Darlene was waiting. She had parked in a handicapped spot and was perched on the front of a 1977 Bonneville like a hood ornament. There was a GPC with at least three inches of ash fused to her lip. She blew him a kiss with lips the color of red paint, then dropped her GPC on the parking lot.

When she stood, the whole car moved and he saw a mess of hair that had been many colors at many different times, though none of those colors ever seemed to fully wash out. Darlene had a solid frame with shoulders as wide as her brother's and a face just as fat.

Wade, almost reluctantly, climbed into her Pontiac and saw a case of warm beer between the seats. A set of pink fuzzy dice hung from the rearview mirror that looked like they'd been dragged behind a garbage truck.

Darlene had him by a good hundred pounds. She told him

she and Ray were twins. Then she pulled from the parking lot in the Bonneville and left dark plumes of smoke behind her.

Wade was nervous and looked over his shoulder. When he asked Darlene where they were going, she didn't tell him. She just handed him a beer, which he accepted and opened and drank. He looked out the window as she rambled and smoked. Told him how she liked it rough. Hinted at the promise of the night that was to come.

She shook pills inside a brown pharmaceutical bottle and asked him if he wanted a bennie.

When they left Algoa, Herb Feeler was behind them. In his four-wheel drive. There was a score to settle and a job to do. Wade Brandt would have to go. Darlene would, too, unfortunately, unless he came up with something better.

Herb Feeler was playing this part by ear, but murder-suicide was an option. It would be a stretch and he knew it—because two suicides in one week was asking a lot of the people—but Herb Feeler was sure he could pull it off. Make it look like Wade Brandt was a psycho. Just another convict society had run through a garbage disposal.

Darlene went to a dump called Bud's Place where the best room in the house was sixty dollars and room service was nonexistent. The television worked when it wanted, and the carpet smelled like hobo piss. But the bed was soft, and he spent the first night doing things to that woman that only three years in prison could make a man do. The first time they made love; he rolled off of her and puked in an ashtray. He told her it was the nine hot Stags he drank on the way to Bud's Place.

The next few pokes went a little smoother, though she was a bit rough with him at times. When she'd said she liked it rough, she had not been lying. Darlene pinned him to the bed and used her size to her advantage. Manhandled him in ways he had not expected—ways reminiscent of how prison life could have been had he not been a fighter, and had he not been protected by the outside world, an advantage spearheading a crank operation inside the joint had afforded him.

Herb Feeler sat in the parking lot and lingered. Watched Wade Brandt go through parked cars after dark and take what he could carry. Herb smoked and listened to country music while he honed his Buck Knife on an Arkansas stone and waited.

He thought about the way things had been going. Once Wade Brandt was dead, Herb was free, and the future belonged to him. The connections he'd made in Jefferson City were finally paying off.

But he could not have something sneak up behind him a year or two down the road. Nor could he have some countrified dip-shit popping up on his radar. Asking for a favor, or threatening to expose him. Herb had worked too hard to see that happen. Any strings connecting him to methamphetamine were cut.

They left Bud's Place the next evening with an extra forty dollars and a hot new pistol. He'd found the gun in a station wagon with a bumper sticker that read TED KENEDDY'S CAR HAS KILLED MORE PEOPLE THAN MY GUN!

He looked in the mirror at the cut above his eye where Darlene had hit him with the ashtray once he'd had enough. She was crazy; he could see it. As he drove, she sat beside him, texting her husband. Telling him who she was with and what she had done.

He rubbed his finger along the cut and took a big gulp of rum. Darlene squeezed his leg and crammed a handful of diet pills down his throat. They'd been eating them nonstop, and that was the primary cause of all that fornicating back at Bud's Place.

Wade raced the Pontiac at a high rate of speed as they blew down the back roads of Gasconade County. He hadn't driven in years, but the wheel felt natural in his hands. This seemed to excite Darlene and she yelled for him to go faster, so Wade jammed the gas pedal to the floor and they listened to the Pontiac choke. The carburetor gagged, and the car pumped an oil cloud of thick black smoke as the motor screamed and pleaded and tried not to blow up.

Everything was fine until they took a corner outside Bland in the wrong lane and the right front tire blew off the rim.

Darlene screeched as the wheel dropped onto the asphalt and began grinding down. Sparks flew up into the window and peppered her big freckled arm.

Wade yelled and yanked the Bonneville to the shoulder.

"My Bonnie," Darlene cried.

He pulled over once they found good shoulder and hoisted the bottle upright. He finished off the rum and asked Darlene if she had a jack.

She grabbed him and hugged him, but he pushed her away and told her she smelled like sweat.

"You got a spare in this beast?"

Darlene said she did, and Wade walked to the back and slid her key in the hole, but Darlene never got out. She fired up a GPC instead and blew a mouthful of smoke out the window.

In the trunk, he found bags of dirty clothes and cat litter and a box filled with sex toys. There were leftover Happy Meals and half-eaten pizzas. He did not see a spare.

"It's there," she promised.

He set the box on the roof and dug a little deeper and found a semi-bald tire under a pile of dirty whites that no amount of laundering could ever sanitize.

He rolled the tire to the front of the car and went back for the jack. The trunk was deep, and it was packed with clothes and trash. The stench of garbage in the afternoon heat took his breath away.

Herb Feeler had followed them in his Dodge Ram. Toothpick between his teeth and a smoke behind his ear. He'd been waiting for his chance to confront them and would give Wade Brandt his terms: return to Algoa for stealing a handgun, or pistols on the shoulder.

Herb knew Wade had a burner. Had watched him swipe it from the wagon.

It was the convict's choice and it did not matter to Herb which decision he made, though a gunfight was right up his alley, and a dead witness was the best kind.

Once that fool had a blowout, Herb saw an opportunity. Set his plan in motion. Pulled up behind Wade and climbed out of the truck and made his way to the Pontiac.

Wade Brandt was on his knees when the sheriff walked up and gave him a hard look with his eyes.

Herb stood in front of the Bonneville, and Wade's pulse hammered his ears.

His mind was on fire from two days of sex and Stag and Benzedrine.

"Y'all's goin' a little fast back there, huh, speedy?"

He looked up and met Herb Feeler's eyes. Said he knew it was a matter of time until he found them.

Sheriff Feeler stood over him as tall as he could like a good ol' boy and grinned. "Didn't take long."

"Now, Herb, I just want you to know that I'm done with that life."

"You think so?"

"I do. Fixin' to go 'n' see my dad right now."

Sheriff Feeler shook his head no.

Wade opened and closed his fists and swallowed hard.

The sheriff read his expression. Held the palm of his hand against the butt of his gun.

Told the outlaw, *Make a move.*

Wade saw the Bronco pull up behind Sheriff Feeler and heard brakes squeal as its driver applied pressure. It came to a stop and parked at an idle with the engine running.

Herb recognized Banks and relaxed his stance, though he kept his hand on the gun.

Banks brought the Bronco to a stop, though he kept it in drive. Foot on the brake, glasspack exhaust rumbling. He said all that was required with the look of unspoiled vengeance he wore so well.

Herb met his eyes and matched Banks an angry scowl of his own. The air was electric. The pressure incredible. Everyone within that odd circle knew they could die.

Wade, on the ground, tire tool in his hand, watched nervously. And waited. And hoped and prayed, after all he had done and been through, not to have it end this way. Not like this. Shot on the side of the road like a dog by the hand of a redneck coward.

Darlene was terrified for the first time in her life. She missed her husband and her kids and their trailer. It wasn't much, but it was theirs. Bought and paid for, and no one could ever take it from them.

How she longed for that security. How, at that moment, no place in the world had ever sounded as appealing. The drone of the river and the boats. Ronnie was dirty, but good. Honest for a meth cook. He was a family man, to the best of his abilities, and he had always loved Darlene.

If she survived the afternoon, she would return to their trailer. Beg Ronnie to take her back. Promise to be a good mom and a good wife and hope he could forgive her.

She was scared and missed home and was no longer having fun.

Herb knew Banks would be a problem, but he had not expected this. Why couldn't the prick have just stayed home? Now it would come down to the thing he never wanted. A shoot-out with a good man who should have kept his mouth shut.

He said, "You dumb—"

Banks drew the cap and ball revolver, quickly and unexpectedly, and fire belched from the barrel and the Bronco filled with smoke. *Now* it was done. Banks used the gun Olen Brandt had planned to give the son who'd died, to save the son who'd lived.

Wade heard the gunshot, and Herb dropped flat on his back. Arms splayed out, hands open. Face smashed in and blackened. A hole had been bored through his forehead that smoke escaped from in a gush.

• • •

Darlene screamed and tried unsuccessfully to heave herself onto the floor. The whole car rocked; the worn-out springs shook and bounced. She was stunned beyond words, with lines of shock etched in her face. She'd seen a man's head blow apart because a lead ball plowed through it.

She held her head in her hands. Crying. Tapping her swollen calves together like a white trash Dorothy Gale.

The smoke was dense, the cloud it formed impenetrable.

It poured heavily from the window of the Bronco. Rose from the body on the pavement in great waves the wind took and carried over the ditch and across the bean field and into the trees.

Banks let off the brake and rolled forward. He could not see out the window. When he pulled away, he saw Wade drag Sheriff Feeler's body to the back of the Pontiac.

Wade stuffed Herb's body in the trunk and slammed the lid. Grabbed the sex toys off the roof and jumped behind the wheel and pulled away gently, careful not to leave any black marks.

He recognized the Bronco and wiped the sweat off his face. Told Darlene they were free—but Darlene was in a state of shock. Told him to take her to her husband.

"It was fun while it lasted," she said. But the ride was over, and she'd had enough.

She told him he could keep the car. She did not want it back. Not after there'd been a dead man inside it.

Wade looked out the rearview mirror and saw smoke. It leaked from the sheriff's head wound and seeped from the trunk and blew across the pavement with the exhaust fumes.

He would dispose of the sheriff in the best place he knew of, a place he had visited many times before. The Tar Hole was an ancient clay pit with four steep walls that grew from pitch-black water of unfathomable depth. A burial ground for a hundred years' worth of collectibles. There were cars and trucks and tractors—even people—who sank to whatever bottom waited all those feet below its dark surface.

Wade Brandt had stolen a tractor-trailer from a truck stop once, and after cleaning out its contents, had driven both the tractor and the trailer into the hole, where it disappeared forever in a thunderous splash, an elongated hiss, and a cloud of boiling steam.

They drove in silence. She never asked about the man in the Bronco or the man in the trunk, and Wade never told her. He just drove her to a gas station and dropped her off and told her she was pretty.

Then he ripped the dice from the rearview mirror and threw them on the road. Limped the car to the fastest speed he dared and removed a butt from the ashtray.

Wiped off the lipstick and relit it and drove her Bonneville to the Tar Hole.

Becky Hastings left Gasconade County in a U-Haul truck with her dad behind the wheel. Her parents had come up from

Florida. She was hurting, and they missed her. She had her mind made up she was leaving, never to return.

She had been a vibrant florist who prided herself on the love she shared through her flowers and her gift baskets. Now she was devastated and heartbroken. She did not know how to feel. Or what to feel. The man she loved was gone. Shot dead in a mobile home by a man who beat his mother.

The thoughts of that. How he had lied to her. What could her man have really been doing? There was money in his car unaccounted for. Drugs. They could not belong to him, not to the man she knew.

She had not been herself since Bo Hastings died.

He had been her world. Her everything. In love since college, she watched him play football and she watched him ride bulls. She was there when that monster threw him. Then she nursed him back to life, convinced him to be a deputy. Refurbish the name his old man had tainted. They had a family to plan and a child to raise.

Now she couldn't get out of bed.

Dale and Jude told her they loved her. She was in their prayers. Jude asked what name Becky would give the baby and she said she would call him Bo. If it was a girl: Billy. After Bo's dad.

She said, "Bo was a good man. Maybe his daddy was, too. Maybe he just got lost."

Banks said that was true. Bo *was* a good man—and yeah, maybe his daddy was, too. Maybe he did get lost. Maybe they both did.

• • •

There was no funeral for Hastings. His mother collected his remains and returned to Saint Louis. What service there had been was private. His mother wanted nothing more than to quietly escape and put the memories of his death behind her.

Banks did not go to the service. Not that he'd been invited. He drove his family to the Brandt farm instead. They had a surprise for the old man and she rode on Grace's lap.

Banks turned on Olen's road and followed waves of drooping fence line. Rough and smooth barked trees. Leafless and bare limbed.

It was a cool day growing colder. Frost had come and killed what it could and wounded everything else.

He parked the Bronco and opened the door and took the puppy from Grace.

"No," she said. "Dah-dee! Puh-pee!"

Jude's and Banks's eyes met. Each smiled. "This is for Olen, puddin', remember?"

"Puh-pee!"

"Hang on, hon. Mama's gotta get you out first."

Jude helped Grace out of her car seat and she cried. Wanted the pup.

Olen walked out the front door and smiled.

"Well, how're you good people doin' today?" he said.

Jude met him with a hug, and Banks watched him smile over her shoulder.

He looked down at Grace. Told her to give Olen the pup. She said no.

"Yeah, sweets, we got that for Olen." She shook her head and said, "Puh-pee."

Jude reached down and took her hand and walked her to Olen. When he saw the pup, there was a small spark of life in his eyes that had dimmed long ago.

Grace refused to give the dog up, and Banks was forced to trick her with some pointing and a sucker and with subtle misdirection. Soon she was sidetracked, walking hand-in-hand with Jude toward the cattle, memories of the pup already fleeting.

Olen stroked the pup's fur, and she shook her fuzzy head and sneezed.

"Good-lookin' pup," he said.

"That she is. She's a bird dog, Olen."

He looked up. Eyebrows arched. "Huntin' dog?"

"Damn straight. What do you say we break her in right? Start takin' her out. Get her used to the sound of gunfire."

Olen put his head down and looked at the walk. Looked up at Banks.

Thank you, he said without words being spoken.

They watched the pup amble toward the shed. Sniff and squat. She walked toward a chicken, then stopped suddenly. Pawed the dirt and pounced.

The chicken jumped, took to flight. The other chickens followed.

"Uh-oh," Olen said.

Beauregard came from the shade at a run and jumped and

came down beside her and pecked her head and ran. A small cloud of dust grew by the shed as the chickens jumped and ran, and the rooster chased the pup around a tree.

Then the pup stopped, and the rooster stopped. Strutted and scratched dirt.

The pup leaped at the rooster and slid into him and pawed.

Beauregard squawked and pecked and ran off to the shade and waited.

Banks and Olen laughed. "She'll fit right in," he said.

Banks nodded. "She sure will. I'm glad to see that."

A sharp northern wind pushed a wall of cold through the low bottoms and the swag.

Banks pointed to a Dodge Ram. "Can't believe you bought a new truck."

Olen smiled and shrugged. "Well, that boy from the insurance company said my old Dodge was kaput. 'Sides, guess it was time for a change. What good's havin' all that money layin' around if you ain't gonna use it?"

"That's right," Banks nodded. "Cuz when you're gone, somebody's goin' to."

"Exactly," Olen said. He looked up at Dale. "And that somebody's gonna be you."

"Huh?"

"When I'm gone, this'll all be yours. I'd like you 'n' your family to have it. I just wanted you to know. Had it drawn up like that for some time. Figured I might as well tell you."

Banks was speechless. There were no words he could say to express his gratitude.

"I really ain't got nobody else to leave it to anyway."

"Well, sure you do. You got that nephew Jackson, don'tchya? And what about Wade? He's out of jail, from what I hear."

Olen laughed. "Neither of 'em's worth two shits 'n' you know it. Besides, that boy of mine, he's lost, 'n' I don't wanna see 'im."

"You never know, Olen. Maybe he's changed."

The old man smiled. "I'd like to think so. Guess time'll tell."

Banks wasn't going to defend him. "Olen, I don't know what to say."

"Don't say nothin'. Just make sure that when I'm gone they lay me beside Arlene."

Banks promised he would.

They watched Jude and Grace talk to the cows. The puppy chased a cat by the barn.

Olen asked Banks about Goat Hill. "What the hell happened up there? I seen fire 'n' black smoke. And what'd them sumbitches do to my truck?"

Banks asked Olen if he knew Butch Pogue.

Olen made a sour face. "I know of that sumbitch. Knowed of his daddy, too. Evil men, both of 'em. There's somethin' ain't never been right about any of them Pogues. Reckon it seems like they all died hard, too. I know Butch done kilt his daddy back in '73. You's still shittin' green back in '73, I reckon."

"Yes, sir."

"The law couldn't prove it, but he done it. Another time he kilt a man with an ax handle, I think it was. That may've been what he done to earn his time in Algoa."

"Well, the one stole your truck was Jerry Dean Skaggs." Banks did not mention the old man's nephew. Even a shit bum like Jackson Brandt deserved a second chance.

Olen recognized the name. "That'n there's the fella they's talkin' 'bout at the Silver Dollar. One shot that bald eagle."

"Yep, that's him, Olen, and he's a real asshole. But it might make you feel better to know either Butch Pogue or his wife carved him up like a Sunday roast."

Olen raised his eyebrows. "*Wife?*"

"Uh-huh. Found Jerry Dean at the bottom of the hill, behind the wheel of your truck. Or what was left of it. Had a big huntin' knife stickin' out of his belly. They liked ta gutted the man, Olen."

"I cain't believe it," he said. "I ain't leavin' the house without my pistol."

"I don't blame you."

Olen frowned at Banks and scratched at his chin. "What's that about a wife? Cain't say as I ever seen or heard of Butch havin' one."

"Really?"

"Now, there was a sister. An older one, I believe. Strange, just like the rest of 'em."

Banks shrugged. He did not tell Olen about the girl who'd been shot or the boy who'd been drowned. The old man's faith in humanity was already fractured. He did not tell him anything more.

Olen excused himself to the house, and Banks grabbed the pup. Walked to the barn and climbed up to the loft. Scurried over old hay bales until he found the bag. But when he opened the bag, it was empty. Banks let it drop to the floor, and his mouth fell open. The money was gone. He searched the loft apprehensively.

This could not be happening.

He climbed back down the ladder and tucked his shirt in and reached down and grabbed the pup. Olen met him in the doorway.

“Find what you was lookin’ for?”

Banks swallowed anxiously and handed him the pup. “She wandered off. Curious little thing.”

“Might have to start lockin’ this door,” the old-timer said.

Olen looked at Banks, but Banks could not meet his eyes.

Jude returned with Grace in her arms and told Banks they were cold.

Banks said OK and shook Olen’s hand. They said their good-byes and left.

The road was fresh with mud, but the sky was blue and cloudless. Banks looked in the rearview mirror and saw Olen leaning up against his truck. He waved.

“Boy, he sure is proud of that truck,” Jude said.

Banks could not hide the grin on his face for all the Skoal in Texas.

“What’s so funny, Dale?”

“Say what?”

“Well, you got this goofy grin on your face right now. What’s so funny?”

The old man had found the money and used it to buy a new truck.

"Oh, nothin', just thinkin' about that old man back there."

She turned and waved. "Look at him, Dale. He loves that thing."

Banks grinned. "Uh-huh."

"You know, I think he'll be just fine, Dale. That old man is quite a character."

Banks told her she was right.

Grace threw the remainder of her sucker onto the console and yelled for the puppy as the Bronco spun in the muck and Banks crossed the cattle guard and pulled onto the road and drove west into a swollen red sun.

MYSTERIOUSPRESS.COM

Otto Penzler, owner of the Mysterious Bookshop in Manhattan, founded the Mysterious Press in 1975. Penzler quickly became known for his outstanding selection of mystery, crime, and suspense books, both from his imprint and in his store. The imprint was devoted to printing the best books in these genres, using fine paper and top dust-jacket artists, as well as offering many limited, signed editions.

Now the Mysterious Press has gone digital, publishing ebooks through **MysteriousPress.com**.

MysteriousPress.com offers readers essential noir and suspense fiction, hard-boiled crime novels, and the latest thrillers from both debut authors and mystery masters. Discover classics and new voices, all from one legendary source.

FIND OUT MORE AT

WWW.MYSTERIOUSPRESS.COM

FOLLOW US:

@emysteries and Facebook.com/MysteriousPressCom

MysteriousPress.com is one of a select group of publishing partners of Open Road Integrated Media, Inc.

CPSIA information can be obtained at www.ICGtesting.com
Printed in the USA
LVOW08s0626110714

393864LV00004B/186/P